The HYSTERICS

KRISTEN HOPE MAZZOLA

The Hysterics

Published: Kristen Hope Mazzola 2015:

Cover Design: by Ari at Cover it! Designs: http://salon.io/#coveritdesigns
Models: Arismar Diaz & Shawn Kirklczuk
Photographer: Mikey Jay Riot
Shoot Director: Steven Vaughn
Formatting by: Kristen Hope Mazzola

Editing by:
C. Marie editingbycmarie@gmail.com
& CJ Pinard

DEDICATION:

To every Fae out there:

Don't ignore your inner Fallon.

PROLOGUE

FAÇADE

FALLON

I was Fallon Dunbar.

I was a drummer.

I was confident, strong, and driven.

I was a junkie.

I am dead.

The full boxes scattered around my small one room apartment made it feel more real. The sinking feeling in the pit of my stomach made it feel so wrong. The new title and job made it feel surreal.

I am Fae Dunham.

I am the assistant editor of Raging Underground.

I am unsure, nervous, and scared shitless.

I am in recovery.

Staring into the full length mirror I had just hung up on the back of the door in my new room, I saw the shell of what I used to be, the life I could no longer have. The only traces left of my old life were the lip piercings I refused to take out. They were my favorites and they were staying. People like me don't get second chances, but for some reason, I was standing knee-deep in one.

There's no turning back now.

I will live again.

CHAPTER ONE

PRACTICE & MEMORIES

DANE

"Hey, man, you all right?" Colt was looking over at me from his seat on his amp.

I gripped the sticks a little tighter in my hands and shook myself from my zone-out. "Yeah. Sorry." I still couldn't get Fae off my damn mind.

Maverick tossed a bottle of water over my toms before swinging his bass guitar's strap back over his shoulder. "Let's take it from the top?"

My sticks clicked quickly, counting out the beat before sending Maverick and myself into a thumping bassline that shot goose bumps up my arms and legs. It felt like I was falling in love every time we started to play; it was *that* exciting.

Finally, the groove settled in nicely and we took off into our newest song, which I was sure would rock our show the next night. It took a while, but an hour and a gallon of sweat later, we were satisfied with how "The Lifespan of a Firefly" sounded.

"This is some great writing, Dane. Why haven't you given us lyrics before?" Rodney holstered the mic and took a swig of his seventh beer while his words slurred a little.

Grabbing a brown bottle out of the fridge, I tried to figure out an answer to his question that didn't make me sound like a complete pussy. "Never thought anything was good enough before, I guess."

Epic fail – that dripped vag all over the place. Way to have a backbone.

"Well, from now on, grow a pair and dish out more of this shit. It's gold. I think we should open with it tomorrow night for sure!"

Colt and Maverick both mumbled and nodded in agreement. My ego felt like it had grown ten times right there on the spot. Being the drummer, I never considered that writing lyrics was something I could be good at. Yeah, I was a journalist. Yeah, I had written angsty teenage poetry when I was younger. But I'd never considered myself an actual writer.

As I slouched onto the worn out couch in Colt's basement, memories rushed over me like warm acid rain.

Beer and sweat were all I could smell as I wiped my dripping forehead with my shirt sleeve. The gentle hum of the Russells' dryer slowly faded in, a little too soft after the booming of our last song left the air.

"Great session, guys." Maverick's weak smile faded as his words lingered in the space. We all knew and we all felt it, but we left it unsaid. There was too much, and no words could make it better; there was nowhere to begin. It was our first practice after the accident a few weeks before and the tension in the air was suffocating us all.

I nodded and choked out, "You guys think we're ready?"

Rodney laughed from the couch, gripping the mic in his hand. "We better be. Like it or not, we're opening tomorrow at Mountain Breath." His faded Zeppelin shirt was starting to wear a hole next to his collar and his lucky Chucks had mud caked on the sides.

"You gonna dress like a bum for it?" Colt joked, opening another beer we'd stolen from his old man's stash. Mr. Russell knew we took them but was usually too loaded to care.

Rodney threw a sweat-soaked towel at Colt right as I stood to stretch out the kink that had been building up in my lower back while I'd sat behind my faded burgundy Ludwin set.

"I think it's going to be sick," I muttered, trying to be enthusiastic and failing miserably.

Maverick clapped me on my back before starting to put his bass in its case. "You ready?"

Digging my keys out of my pocket, I stared at my sticks where they rested in their bag attached to my floor tom. I stood up gradually from my stool, starting to make my way to the stairs. "Yeah. Let's head home."

"Get a good night's sleep, gents! Tomorrow is going to be epic!" Rodney called up to us from the bottom of the stairs, a sly grin fixed firmly on his face. He had no fucking idea what he was asking of Mav and me, and it was better off that way.

The sound of a beer opening in my ear and the feel of cold suds spraying on my neck and cheek snapped me back to real time. Rodney erupted into a fit of laughter next to me.

"What the hell, man?" I thrashed, wiping my face off with the bottom of my shirt.

"Come on. I couldn't resist. You were zoning out again."

Colt sat in a metal folding chair across the faded lime green carpet, laying his guitar down next to him. "You all right, Dane? You've been spacey all night."

"Yeah, man. I'm fine."

I got up and started to make my way up the stairs to take a piss. Right as I opened the basement door, I heard Maverick say in a low voice, "Guys, it's April thirteenth. You know how he gets around this time."

My stomach sank. He was right. The twentieth was coming too fast for me to keep up with, and the memories and dreams were getting worse by the day.

Deep breaths.

Easier said than done.

Time would pass and it would still be hard, but I was still breathing.

Fuck it.

As I walked into the living room, trying to make it into the back hallway undetected by Colt's parents, I heard crying coming from the couch.

Turning on my heels, I found Sheila Russell sobbing into a pillow. When I cleared my throat, she popped her head up, startled by my presence.

"Sheils? You all right?" I looked down at Colt's kid sister, who was definitely not a kid anymore.

Before, she'd been pimply-faced, chunky, and awkward. Now, her face had cleared, she'd hired a personal trainer, and her degree in Mass Communications was helping her break out of her shell, to say the least. She was stunning in her own way. Not my type, but still pretty.

"Yeah." She sniffed. "I just got turned down for an awesome summer internship. It's the only one I applied for and that's biting me in the butt now." She tried to laugh it off, but her eyes stayed sad.

"You know the saying, Sheils."

She rolled her eyes and mumbled, "Don't put all your eggs in one basket."

I laughed, nodded, and gave her a tight squeeze as I continued on before my bladder busted. While I was trotting over to the half bath down the hall, Sheila called to me, "Thanks, Dane."

"Don't mention it! Call Julie. Schedule a mani-pedi date like the old days and you'll be good as new!" I yelled back before slamming the door shut behind me, barely able to get my zipper down before I pissed myself.

CHAPTER TWO

IT BEGINS

FALLON

The color drained from my hair as I watched the blackish muck mix with the water swirling around my feet. My light auburn was now cloaked in a midnight black. The freckles that dotted my skin and the lightness of my hazel eyes were still dead giveaways as to who I really was. Add in all of my tattoos and the giant chip on my shoulder and there was no mistaking my identity. All I could do was hope that during my meeting with my new boss and longtime family friend on Monday, the glasses, hair, and articulated speech would be enough.

Not too long ago, I'd woken up from a three-day binge in a hospital room after an overdose and decided enough was enough. I'd quit the band and moved back in with good old mom and stepdad.

The "I told you so" speeches were a small price to pay for having almost taken their only child out of this world. Luckily, my *real* dad's college roommate had decided to give me a shot. Payton

Downing was taking a huge risk when it came to hiring me. For most of my childhood Payton had been like an uncle to me, but what I was asking for was more than any family member should have to do. Even so, the answer had been yes, without question, and I was getting a fresh start with a job I could have only dreamed of.

Thankfully, I'd had enough sense in my early twenties to finish college online while touring with my band all over Canada and the US for three years. Between the recreational drugs and rock and roll, I didn't know how I'd passed, but I had managed. Cs get degrees, after all.

My resume was less than polished with a cocaine overdose, years of touring with a punk band, and a few brushes with the law staining the white paper that was filled with columns I'd had published, my college degree, and my amazing ability to clean up well.

This was my second chance, my fresh start, and staring into my reflection in the mirror terrified me.

What if I fuck this one up, too?

DANE

"All right, everyone. Settle down." Payton, my overly cheery, overly plump boss bounded into our meeting room, his glasses falling down his nose as he carried a huge stack of papers. "As you all know, over the last year our little online chronicle has sparked a wildfire. Needless to say, I need help. *We* need help. So I have hired an assistant editor. Her name is Fae Dunham, and she'll be joining us shortly."

He paused for what I figured to be dramatic effect while crickets took over the room. We were all grungy musicians playing journalist to support our passionate habit. We enjoyed our lack of leadership and censorship, and no snobby outsider was going to change that.

I sat opposite Payton with my feet up on the large oval conference table while all my coworkers sat wide-eyed, like deer in Mack truck lights. I chuckled, sipping steaming coffee out of my Hysterics travel mug.

"Mr. Pearson? Care to share with the rest of us what is so funny?" Payton shoved his glasses back up his face, pausing halfway through organizing and passing out the papers that were now spread out in front of him.

I shook my head.

Crickets. They were all just sitting there, glancing at one another like I was about to be sent to the principal's office.

I cleared my throat. "I just don't see why—" *Whoa.* Mid-sentence, I was completely taken aback by one of the most incredible sights I had ever seen in my life.

She slowly walked in after opening the door, trying to enter without interrupting the meeting. Her dark black hair was curtaining her slender, pale, freckle-ridden face. Thick, black-rimmed glasses sat cutely on her nose, which looked at least a size too big for her face. A soft blush dusted her high cheekbones as her light pink lips pursed together. She rested a small hand on Payton's shoulder. A tight-fitting pantsuit hugged her subtle curves while just a hint of ink peeked out from under the jacket sleeve on her left arm.

Payton's eyes darted from glaring at me to lighting up with a huge smile as he glanced over his shoulder at the gorgeous newcomer—not like a boss usually would, but like a loving uncle looking at a favored niece. "Everyone, please give a warm welcome to the newest member of our staff and your new boss, Fae."

She slowly let her lips crane into a nervous smile as she waved. "Hello."

Her lips were incredible; I couldn't stop staring at them: full and luscious with two hooped rings that begged for my tongue to taste and my teeth to bite.

Her voice was a whisper as she glanced around the room. "I am truly looking forward to getting to know you all."

Fae couldn't be more than a few years younger than I was. There was something in her eyes that didn't quite add up, a sadness battling something I couldn't put my finger on; it was intoxicating and magnetically intriguing.

CHAPTER THREE

LIQUID COURAGE – ONE MONTH LATER

FALLON

Looking down at the blue ink on my hand, smudged almost enough to be illegible, I realized I'd finally found the place. I pulled my black trench coat tighter, cinching the belt again. I could not imagine that this was one of the better neighborhoods around, and I was shocked I'd even had the balls to show up at all. But a new life meant new adventures and having to step out of my comfort zone just a little.

Two girls bounced by me, clinging together, probably to protect themselves from the chilly wind and light drizzle of rain. Even in late April, I could feel the city's cold deep down into my bones. After tripping slightly in a puddle and damning the six-inch heels I had stupidly worn, I grabbed the door that the others rushed into.

Dane had been right, I was shocked by the venue. I walked to the second floor of a packed scene. It was dark, smoky, and erupting with the roar of half-drunk people crowding everywhere. The stage had a light reddish glow that barely made the three guitars and drum set visible from where I'd entered.

After checking my coat, I was able to shove my way down the stairs and over to the bar faster than I had expected and happily flagged down a tall, dark-haired bartender with an incredible phoenix tattoo on his forearm. I yelled my order to him over the shrieks of drunken fangirls.

A moment later, I heard the band's lead singer scream into the microphone, "Ladies, ladies, calm down. We're The Hysterics, and we're here for you. Please be so kind as to welcome my awesome bandmates. We have Dane on the drums."

The crowd exploded. After pausing for the noise to die down, the frontman continued as Dane's sweet smile lit up.

"Maverick on the bass."

He started to play a light thumping rhythm at the sound of his name, which Dane jumped on, too.

"Colt is over there, ladies, on lead guitar."

Colt's face had a devilish grin on it as he started to play along with Maverick's tempo.

"And I'm Rodney."

With that, the crowd went wild and the band kicked off with the melody of an upbeat number that was quickly winning over the crowd.

Rodney was a terrific frontman, playing guitar and singing while practically having sex with any woman he made eye contact with. It was amazing to be out at a show, watching a fantastic band play, but my mind kept jumping back to the bitter guilt and jealousy that I was riddled with. I grabbed my beer in one hand, slamming down the shot of tequila with the other.

Liquid courage, here I come.

It was my first time being around live music since I'd quit my band. It was thrilling and terrifying. I wanted to run away and jump on stage all at once.

"Calm down, crazy lady. Enjoy the ride." The sound of my best friend Starr's voice echoed in my head while I made my way to the side of the stage closest to where Dane was. I was in awe as I got a better look at his gorgeous black DW drum set, to the point of almost drooling. I missed playing so much that it almost hurt.

I took a swig of my beer just as a ballad started to sway the mood down a little. While Dane waited for his cue to jump into the song, we made eye contact. His smile was brilliant. Even his eyes seemed to smile when our gazes met. Right then, I realized how attractive he was.

No more musicians. Don't do it.

That stupid voice in my head was annoying, but right. I'd had my own freaking Jiminy Cricket chirping in my ear ever since I had woken up in that damn hospital bed.

All the band members were attractive in their own way. Rodney was tall and skinny, with sandy brown hair and the whitest teeth I had ever seen. Maverick was a little bit shorter, but from the definition of his muscles under his shirt, I could tell how hard he worked for an awesome body. Colt was sweet looking with kind of a baby face, but when he smiled, I could see all of the sins he was proud of spreading across his face. Then there was Dane. He had jet black hair, was the only band member with visible tattoos covering both of his arms, and had the best smile I had ever laid eyes on.

I danced and swayed to their music for the whole set, never leaving my spot, not even for another drink. I really couldn't believe how great they were, almost like New Found Glory meets Rage Against the Machine. *If that's even possible.*

I was in love.

"Encore! Encore!"

The roaring fans and I were in agreement that the show should go on.

But, like all good things, they freaking ended. Rodney said goodnight and apologized to the protesting fans, explaining that they had to make room for the next band to come on. As the guys started to break down, Dane mouthed to me to wait one second while holding his finger up and flashing that killer smile.

Oh yeah. Weak knees.

He then turned to Maverick and pointed at me, mouthing something else. The next thing I knew, Maverick had jumped off the stage and was right next to me. He introduced himself by yelling into my ear and then helped me up onto the stage to join the band. I was so embarrassed because my dress was almost exposing my underwear the first time I was meeting Dane's band members, but they didn't seem to notice.

Dane grabbed my hand as I got to my feet and shouted, "You look freaking awesome, Fae! Thanks for showing up."

I felt my cheeks burn red and yelled back, "This place is amazing! Thanks for inviting me."

He motioned toward backstage. "Want a drink?"

I nodded and followed him away from the still screaming fans. Once inside the band's dressing room—which was about the size of a closet—I really got nervous. Dane introduced me to everyone and they all seemed so nice. I was shocked. Most of the musicians I knew back home and from tour who were at almost-star-level like The Hysterics were jerks.

Tossing me a beer, Maverick queried, "So, Fae, right?"

I nodded.

"How'd you meet our boy here?" He clapped Dane on the shoulder.

Before I could go into the story, Dane noticed my nervousness and answered for me. "She's my new boss." Dane winked at me and I relaxed a little. "Well, kind of. I'm the new assistant editor at Raging Underground. I've only been in Chicago for a little while now." Talking about myself was unsettling. I wasn't used to being Fae Dunham yet, so I took a long swig of my beer and started to rave about how impressed I was with them, hoping I could find some courage in the bottom of the bottle and stop blushing. "When Dane told me that his band had a gig and he wanted me to come check it out, I had no idea it would be of this caliber. Seriously, you guys killed it out there."

"You're sweet," Rodney pitched over my way while lightly picking at his Baby Taylor. "Dane, nice job bringing a chick around that doesn't act like a bitch or a gushing groupie."

Through a nervous chuckle, Dane leaned over and said into my ear, "Don't mind him. Wanna go check out the next group? I heard they are pretty awesome."

"Sure, that'd be great."

Grabbing my hand, Dane led me out of the room as I waved goodbye to the others. They were all polite and told me to come back again. As we walked down the hall, a few girls eyed me with jealousy written all over their faces, some of them even cooing their hellos to Dane as sensually as possible. To my surprise, his grip on my hand got tighter and he pulled me into his side, ignoring the floozies. When we made our way to the bar, I ordered us a round of water. Dane's eyes lit up with a twinge of curiosity as we drank our nonalcoholic beverages. I needed to keep my head about me and not let booze start making decisions for me. Staying sober was a safer course than risking betraying my inner Jiminy Cricket.

"Thanks for coming out. I didn't think you would make it." Dane's voice was straining to be louder than the heavy metal on stage and the fans' excited shrills.

"I really missed this type of stuff. I loved your kit, by the way!" My eyes met his and I realized I was getting dangerously close to blowing part of my cover.

No one can know I am a drummer. I had to remind myself of this sometimes. It was like being a fish and trying to convince people I was a mermaid—it just didn't make sense.

I cursed under my breath; thankfully, my mumbles got swallowed up by the crowded room.

"Oh yeah," Dane chuckled. "She's pretty great. You been around a lot of bands before?"

His mouth curled into an extremely sexy half smile as I fumbled for words, his gray eyes piercing mine.

Fuck, he's so damn hot.

"I dabbled in a little bit of music journalism in college. Payton wouldn't hire just anyone, would he?"

Dane shook his head, tightly pulling me into him. He pressed my back up against his chest, moving to the music. We danced right next to the bar for the rest of the band's set. The other members of The Hysterics had joined us and ordered a few more drinks while we enjoyed the fast-paced rhythm and near screaming of the lead singer.

Eventually, Dane and I found ourselves alone again at the beginning of another band's second song. The rest of his bandmates had trickled off into the shadows with some wannabe groupies. I was relieved when the song started calming down into a ballad and Dane took me into his strong, tattooed arms again. We slow danced and his lips brushed my ear ever so softly, sending chills up my spine.

He breathed gently into my neck, "Do you want to get out of here?"

I playfully shook my head as he kissed my neck once. I was enjoying myself, but this was enough playtime outside my comfort zone for one night.

I pulled away from him, just enough to look into his smoldering steel eyes. "You should ask me out on a real date before you think I am going to 'get out of here with you,' Romeo," I said, making air quotes and grinning.

He nodded, smiled. After grabbing my trench coat, he escorted me out of the packed club. My inner Jiminy was screaming at me to stop playing with fire again, but I was a moth drawn to a flaming hot drummer.

We waited on the curb for a taxi to drive by and he hailed one for me. Before releasing my hand, he rested his cheek on mine. "I'll see you at work tomorrow. How about drinks after with the guys? They seemed to want you to come around again soon."

I nodded, giggling a little, feeling his stubble graze my face. "That's still not a date," I teased, whispering in his ear.

He tightened his grip around my waist, getting his lips within half an inch of mine. "I know. How about dinner after we meet up with the guys?"

Without waiting for my answer, he pressed his lips to mine, and I was stunned. I gently pushed Dane away, making sure to keep sweet eye contact with him.

"It's a date then." I smirked, a little breathless from our kiss.

"See you at work, drummer boy."

With that, I was in the cab, speeding away to a sleepless night, too excited about what the Windy City was going to have in store for me after all.

DANE

Even though the lights were nearly off, I could feel the energy of the deafening horde growing with anticipation. I reached down to find my fresh pair of sticks, firmly grasping them in my right hand. The smooth, black paint on the wood was sleek and intoxicating as I twirled them in my fingers.

Fuck yeah. This is going to be a good night.

Sweat was already starting to form on my brow as the adrenaline coursed through my veins. My breath started to quicken and my heart felt like it was going to explode out of my chest. Even though I had been on stage with these guys every weekend for years, each gig sent an overwhelming feeling rushing over me, reminding me why I truly loved what I did.

The lights started to brighten and the spotlight lit up Rodney's face. All of the booze-fueled fans screeched as Rodney started his usual introduction.

"Ladies, ladies, calm down. We're The Hysterics, and we're here for you. Please be so kind as to welcome my awesome bandmates. We have Dane on the drums."

I heard my cue and let a stick twirl in the light above my

head before stomping out the bass rhythm for the remainder of the band to be introduced. The crowd erupted and we dove right into the newest tune I'd written.

Rodney's voice was smooth and lustful, unknowing of the truth that burned bright in the words that dripped from his lips like honey on a hot summer's day. My mind flashed to the tattoo on my shoulder: two small fireflies, one protecting the other. My heart stopped and my breath caught as she crossed my mind and everything around me stopped for a brief moment.

It's a dull kind of pain that just sits in my heart and weighs me down

And you're the only one who can fix it

It burns and erupts at the worst times

Stinging old wounds that have already been licked clean

Right when headway is made, the darkness crashes again

Closing in on my starlight

Little flicks of magic extinguished one by one

The firefly's lifespan gets tested over and over

Thankfully, she is inked into existence for all eternity

Once the set was over, I started to pack up the equipment and Mav helped me get Fae up on the stage. She seemed pretty happy with the show and comfortable with the guys, which surprised them all. Maybe it was that she was new to the city, but most girls from around here got a little unnecessarily star struck around us. Fae was calm while complimenting us on our set. She used biz words like they were common, but I shrugged them off until I was standing next to her at the bar.

She called my drum set a "kit", and that was it.

I had to shout over the crowd's roars. "Oh yeah!" I couldn't help but laugh at her compliment of the DW. "She's pretty great. You been around a lot of bands before?"

Right then the world stopped around me. I was standing in front of Fallon Dunbar, the former drummer of Regicide Assisted, a band that had just broken up because rumor had it their drummer had died from an overdose of coke. She was a legend in the underground circuit, but she had flown in under my radar. I decided to not let Fae—Fallon – know I'd figured out her alter ego and went along with the sheer surprise of standing in the presence of an awesome chick.

I tested my luck and was completely shot down. I figured she had met too many jackass musicians on the road and decided to not become another one. We danced and listened to my friend's band play a few songs until I finally was able to get her alone on the street. I pressed my hand on the small of her back and brought her in for one hell of a kiss. Her lips were so soft and she tasted like sheer fuckable magic, not to mention how incredible her lip rings felt gliding over my bottom lip.

As I watched her speed away in the taxi, I had a newfound excitement to quickly get through work that next day. Since the band met up for drinks after work pretty much every day, I figured it would be a nice icebreaker into a date. I wasn't really the dating type, but if Miss Fallon Dunbar wanted to play all goody two-shoes, I figured I should play along.

I made my way back over to where Colt and Rodney were standing, trying to get the attention of a tall tattooed guy behind the bar.

Colt leaned close to my ear. "Where'd the chick go? She was

hot."

I smiled and shook my head, laughing. "She went home. Playing hard to get, I guess. She's gonna hang out with us tomorrow."

Colt smiled mischievously and I knew the idea of Fae-Fallon—whatever I was supposed to think of her as—naked was crossing his mind, which pissed me off.

"Dude, I just made out with her!" I yelled loud enough for the entire club to hear if they wanted, but Colt and Rodney were the only ones who seemed to let the greatness register.

Rodney punched my shoulder. "Fuck yeah, man." Then he took a shot of vodka and wandered off with a tall blonde who was wearing enough makeup for an entire brothel.

Two giggling blonde girls walked up to Colt and me as the bartender finally took my order. I waved the girls in Colt's direction and he slunk into the shadows with both clinging onto each of his arms.

"So, where's your lady friend? Fae?" Maverick was standing next to me, a mixed drink wrapped in a white napkin in his hand.

He was more than a bandmate or even a friend. He was my brother, or at least the closest thing I had to family. He knew something was up with me, I could see it in his face.

"She hopped in a cab and headed home. Work early in the morning, ya know."

He nodded. "Ain't that a bitch?"

"I gotta tell you something, promise not to say anything?"

He held up three fingers. "Scout's honor."

I leaned in and loudly said, "She's not just any chick. She's fucking Fallon Dunbar!"

I let it sink in and watched as the words clicked. His eyes grew about ten times bigger as he punched my shoulder.

"Fuck, dude!"

"Yeah, tell me about it!" I chugged the rest of my beer, slamming the empty glass onto the bar top.

"All I can say is, don't fuck that one up!"

I could always count on Mav to be Captain Obvious. I chuckled, "Yeah, man. No *shit!* Don't tell the guys. Or anyone."

"Don't worry. Your secret—well, her secret—is safe with me."

CHAPTER FOUR

THE MEETING

DANE

Usually after a gig, I pass the hell out right after a shower. Tonight, there was no way that was going to happen. I was consumed with replaying kissing Fallon over and over. It was a short kiss, no tongue, just simple, quick, and perfect. I felt like a freaking preteen girl giggling in a corner after having made out with her crush for the first time.

I finally fell asleep around four in the morning, and my alarm screamed at six thirty.

Ugh. Fuck, it's early.

I desperately wanted to roll over and keep sleeping, but Fallon had called the entire staff in for a meeting and there was no fucking way I was going to be late for that. I shaved, brewed coffee, put on a button-down and tie, and headed out the door twenty minutes early.

With my oversized travel mug in hand, I walked into the office and an all-too familiar voice cooed behind me, "What's the special occasion, hot stuff?"

Whitney was standing way too close for comfort. She was the only chick I'd ever brought home from work. *Huge mistake.* She had a banging body: tight ass, long, blonde hair, a huge mouth she knew how to work well. But, she was a leech. All she did was gossip and talk shit. Not my scene. I'd only kept her around for a little while because she'd been a no-strings-attached fuck. Now she wanted strings, and I wanted nothing to do with her.

"Trying to act the part, I guess." I dismissed her and continued to walk toward the conference room.

There was no way my dick was going to go near her again, not after having kissed Fallon. One kiss, that's all it had taken. Those few seconds with her had been worth more than all the hours I'd spent with that shallow slut.

I could feel my heart skip when I heard Fallon's sweet voice coming from around the corner. Then I quickly kicked myself for how sappy I had become in the last twenty-four hours.

Dude, get a grip. She's just a chick.

Sitting back in my chair in the meeting room, I smiled as all my fellow writers slowly trickled in, tired, coffee in hand. I could see the confusion and frustration on their faces. Every once in a while, we had a meeting, but never at eight in the morning. Most of us were musicians or insane music fanatics, keeping vampire-like schedules and hating the term 'morning'. It was part of the reason why the online chronicle idea was an awesome job choice—the hours were appealing.

Ever since Fallon Dunbar had become our assistant editor, structure had been creeping in, denying our resistance with a devil's laugh. Payton had called the meeting knowing full well how unpopular it was going to be with the staff, but he was trying to make big changes in the chronicle and Fallon was right smack dab in the center of it all. And I was enamored.

Fallon was hot in every way possible. She was strong, an amazingly talented writer, and covered in the hottest tattoos I had ever seen on a chick. The best part was how much she was a mystery to me. She was one of the most talented underground drummers I have ever heard of; she was supposed to be dead, but here she was, showing up in my life like an archangel, her wings still a little singed from the wreckage of her past. I figured no one else had put the connection together about our new editor's true identity, and I knew that's what Fallon wanted.

Fallon beat most of the staff into the room. A lot of them were lingering in the hall or shuffling papers on their desks before the meeting was supposed to start. Even with her sleepy eyes, Fallon was stunning in her tight, black dress pants, her thick-framed glasses, and a flowing teal top, her hair thrown up. I couldn't help but stare.

She draped her suit jacket over the back of a chair before gliding over to me, half smiling as she glanced at her watch. "We have, like, fifteen minutes before we have to start." She pulled a chair close to mine and straddled it backwards. "How're you doing, Dane?"

Her lips were a succulent red that my body ached to taste again. I stuttered for words, but I kept them at a level whisper, playing off my lustful attraction as best as I could.

"I'll be better once we have that date you made me promise to take you on." I forced my lips to curl into a smile, trying not to blush, being careful to not let my eyes slide down to her perfect tits, which were playing peekaboo with her almost see-through top.

She ran her fingers through her hair, tucking a few stragglers into her messy bun and biting her lip into a half smile. "Well, then, we will just..." She trailed off as Payton strode into the room.

Fallon tossed a playful pout over at me without finishing her sentence. She slowly started to rise, probably noticing that the last two members of our writing staff had scrambled through the door. I looked at her, pretending to sulk a little, and then nodded, mouthing "We'll talk later" at her with a wink.

I tried to pay attention while Fallon strolled through how well our fans were responding to our articles and how much more emotion we could bleed from our passion for the music we were writing about. All of it was interesting, but nothing could pull my mind from cracking her mystery.

Why is she so secretive? Why doesn't she want anyone to know who she is, how talented she is?

CHAPTER FIVE

ROMEO

FALLON

Fresh coffee.

There was nothing better. The smell of warm hazelnut wafted up as I poured yet another cup into the bright pink mug Starr had made for me a few Christmases ago. Scrolled across it was my favorite of Hemingway's famous quotes: "There is nothing to writing. All you do is sit down at a typewriter and bleed." And in the bottom of the mug, only visible once the coffee was gone, the words 'Love ya, bitch!' were printed in bold. It always made me smile when I thought about how excited she had been to give me the stupid thing.

Fuck, I miss her!

I glanced at my watch. It was only one in the afternoon, and I had probably already guzzled down an entire pot.

"Top me off?" Dane was standing next to me in the break area.

I filled up his mug. "Sure thing."

His smile.

His eyes.

His fitted gray button-down and black silk tie.

Licking him from head to toe crossed my mind as I almost overflowed his cup.

His voice was low and gruff. "So, we still on for tonight?"

I need to get away from him before I jump him right here.

Starting to walk away, I tossed over my shoulder, "Sure thing, Romeo." I giggled a little to myself, remembering how fantastic his lips felt right as my boss's big rosy cheeks came into my view.

"Ah, Fal—er, Fae. Right on time, I like that." He smiled and gestured for me to take a seat as he closed his office door.

I crossed my legs nervously, wondering why my boss had texted me on my way back to work from lunch, asking me to drop in his office right when I got into the building.

"You wanted to see me, sir?" I failed miserably at hiding my nerves as my voice shook.

"Yes. I wanted to see how you're adapting to the office and staff." His voice was cheery as he glanced over the mountain of paperwork covering his desk. "Everything going smoothly, my dear? And cut that *sir* crap out." Payton winked, leaning back into his dark brown leather chair as it moaned under his weight.

I relaxed into the plush armchair under me. "I love it here!" I blurted out.

With a warm chuckle, he slapped his desk. "Fantastic. Are we on schedule for today's deadline? I want all articles posted promptly at seven p.m."

"Yes. Everything will be ready and waiting by five for your review. All I will have to do is hit publish at seven once I get your go-ahead."

"Wonderful. Then I best let you get to sifting through all those articles."

I made my way to the closed office door, stopping just short of it. "Payton?"

"Yes, *Fae*?" He winced as my fake name hung in the air. I could tell that he, too, was having a hard time getting used to it.

I whispered, "Thank you."

His brow creased questioningly as he waited for an explanation.

I looked down at my suit jacket's sleeves, which were covering up most of my tattoos, only letting a little wisp of color escape on my left wrist. "For giving me this chance."

"Everyone deserves a second chance, Fallon. Even you." His face spread into a warm, loving grin and I walked out of his office, the tiniest hint of a tear rolling down my cheek.

I wish I could believe that.

While editing a terrible article about the 'new age revolution of music sweeping the nation' that felt like it had been written by a third grader, a soft knock rapped on my open office door. Without looking away from my computer screen, which was riddled with purple and blue edits all over the open Word document, I called, "Yes?"

"Fae? I have a late submission for you." Dane's voice came whispering through the stale room like a breath of fresh air. I looked up to see him walking into my office with a piece of paper gripped in his hands. "Great. It'll give me a break from this piece of you-know-what." I rolled my eyes as I grabbed the page from Dane, shoving my fake glasses back onto my face. I hated them, but I felt like they made me look more the part of a literary assistant editor.

"It's a shameless plug, but I think it's worth its salt."

He took a seat while I started reading "It Changes You" by Dane Pearson.

There is nothing better than the feeling of the music seeping into your pores. That one moment when it all makes sense and the world melts into nothingness. It engulfs you. It changes you. It becomes you. It saved me.

"This is really good, Dane." I smiled up at him to see the spark of a shy grin start to take over his nervous face.

"Really?"

I nodded. "Email it to me? I'll get it ready for the posting tonight."

He practically jumped out of his seat. "You'll have it in two seconds. Mountain Breath at eight?"

I smirked. "If Payton doesn't keep me too late, I'll be there."

With a swift wink and a small, seductive smile topped off with a lower lip bite, he was out the door.

Damn, he's too hot. I need to kiss those lips again.

I wanted to call him back into the office and throw him onto my desk. That would be way too inappropriate. *But so much fun.*

"Looks like an HR violation," I heard a mousy voice cackle

from the hall as a giggle followed.

I was able to catch a glimpse of Whitney Quints as her blonde ponytail bobbed away from my office next to a short, skinny brunette I couldn't remember the name of to save my life.

CHAPTER SIX

BLACKOUT ON THE MOUNTAIN

FALLON

Finally. I stretched, grabbed my bag, and locked my office door. It was almost nine already, but all of the articles were perfect and submitted, and the rest were ready for the morning.

Payton signaled a cab and opened the door for me. "Great work today, Fae. See you tomorrow bright and early."

I waved goodbye to him as the cabbie asked, "Where to, miss?" in an accent I couldn't quite place.

"Er, I think the name of it is Mountain something?"

Shit, why can't I remember what Dane said? I should have had him write it down or text it to me before he left the office.

He chuckled. "Are you meeting musicians by any chance?"

"Yeah. How'd you know?"

"Lucky guess. A big group head to Mountain Breath on Third

a few times a week. They have open mic night on Thursdays."

"That's the place!"

The drive didn't take long, and soon I was tipping the cabdriver and making my way into a dimly lit bar that resembled more of a hallway than anything else. I craned my neck over the packed bar toward a small stage with a backless barstool and a microphone set up under a spotlight. Sitting at a table right next to the stage were Dane and Maverick. After shoving through the crowd of people, I finally made my way over to them.

Dane jumped up with a stupidly giddy grin sweeping across his face. "You made it!" he shouted over the rumbling of the bar patrons.

I nodded and mouthed "Hi" to Maverick before he got up and gave me one of those dude-half-hug-things. I took my seat across from Dane as he waved to a tall server with long, straw-colored barrel curls that were almost touching her ass. She bounced over and plopped right on Dane's lap without any hesitation. A sharp bite of jealousy hit my stomach as I pictured throwing the bleached blonde – with her corset that was two sizes too small for her fake rack – off Dane's lap, gripping his face, and claiming his lips for my own again. My face must have given my thoughts away because Dane hurriedly cleared his throat and shifted her off him.

With a frown, she stood and looked over to me. "What do you want?" she snapped.

The bite in her voice and the look of disgust that infected her once perky smile gave me more pleasure than it should have.

"Just a light beer please." I smiled as sweetly as I could while I watched her walk to the bar to get my drink.

Dane looked right into my eyes, nervously rubbing the back of his neck. "She's been pulling that shit with all of us since she started working here."

Maverick nodded. "Yup. A wannabe if I've ever seen one."

Play dumb. It'll help keep this charade up.

"Wannabe what?" I questioned, pretty sure of the answer, but I wasn't supposed to be from their world. "Ugh. It wasn't until we started playing bigger clubs that groupies started to be so forward and annoying. They just want to be around on the off chance that we'll become famous and then they can brag about their band whore rating."

I couldn't help but laugh extremely loudly at how sincere and disgusted Maverick was while he made that statement. "I guess a band whore rating is like a badge of honor for slutty groupies, huh?"

A beer bottle slammed down next to me and I glanced up just in time to see that terrible look still plastered on our server's face.

"Well, I guess I offended someone."

Maverick glanced over at the huffing server while she glared over in my direction. "Yeah, looks that way," he chuckled.

I winked at Dane as he shrugged. His voice was gravelly as his voice strained to be louder than the crowd. "Some people hate hearing the truth. I, on the other hand, prefer it."

Before I could think too much about Dane's comment and hope that it hadn't been directed at my true identity, a heavyset woman heaved onto the stage and grabbed the mic.

"First up, we have Candice Davenport accompanied by Maverick Steele."

The bar clapped and cheered as Maverick shoved away from the table. "Wish me luck, guys. I haven't played with this one in a while."

Dane and I both clapped enthusiastically. I switched to

Maverick's seat, supposedly to have a better view of the stage, but really just to be closer to Dane.

"What's this all about? How does the open mic work here?"

Dane leaned in closer than necessary to explain, lightly resting his hand on my thigh. "Maverick is an awesome musician, and when singers come in who don't have backup, he'll step in. I don't think he's ever gotten a song request he didn't know."

"Wow. That's impressive."

Dane smiled. "Yeah. Sure is!" After another swig of beer, he continued. "We've been coming here since we were kids. Actually, our first show was right up on that stage."

Maverick took a seat on the stool behind a kind-faced woman in her mid-twenties. They chatted for a second before the chick started to speak in a meek voice.

"Hi, everyone! I'm Candice, and I am going to sing 'Our Song' by The Spill Canvas."

Maverick started fingerpicking one of my favorite songs of all time as Candice jumped in right on time with a raw but beautiful timbre that sent chills down my spine. I started singing along without even realizing it.

Dane scooted his chair closer to mine so our seats were touching then whispered in my ear, "You look beautiful tonight, by the way."

I shot him a coy smile and kissed him on the cheek. "Thanks."

With a playful smirk, he leaned in a little closer. "For what?"

"For this, for helping me feel welcome in a scary new city where I know no one and have no friends."

"Well that's a lie. We're your friends."

Right as his lips were about to connect to the nape of my neck, I felt his shoulder get pushed into mine as Rodney chimed in, "Yeah, we're all great friends here."

Rodney took his seat with Colt not too far behind and gestured to the waitress to bring another round of drinks. Colt sat down next to me after dragging another seat over for Maverick once he was done with the next singer. We chatted about why they had taken so long to join us, and then the room started to spin around me. Everything went into a blur when I heard lyrics I had written whisk through the bar. My blood went cold as a soft male voice mused words that had bled from my soul just a few short years before.

In the stillness, you'll find me

In the noise and confusion, you'll haunt me

A fine line gets walked

Inside the divine mind of frenzy

Tread lightly, only whisper

There might be just a glimmer

I want to break down, stop this hiding

But revealing is maddening, the unknown faltering

Charting new courses should be exciting

There's a depth most unwilling to enter

But the path less traveled may lead to splendor

"Fae?" a faint voice called to me. "Fae, wake up."

I breathed in sharply, inhaling the terrible aroma of beer and piss as I opened my eyes to harsh bright lights. "What? What's going on?"

Dane's face slowly started to come into focus while he held my body in a sitting position on the bathroom counter of Mountain Breath. "You passed out. Are you feeling okay?"

I nodded, but what a load of shit that was. My heart was racing, and so was my mind. The last thing I could remember was hearing my words haunt me.

"Well, I think it's time to get you out of here. It's been a long day."

I nodded again. I felt like a fool, but that was all my body could do at that point. Overwhelmed would be an understatement for how I'd felt right then. I had been completely unprepared for those situations to come up. I knew that my band had been pretty popular and I was bound to run into it at some point—on the radio at the gym, someone posting something on social media, something coming up at work about their hunt for a new drummer going south and the band breaking up. Yeah, that was true. I was the sole reason for a very promising band that was about to make it big time crashing and burning in an all too cliché way: drugs.

Dane hailed a cab, opened the door, and slid in, all while holding my hand and helping me into the car.

"Where to?" the cabbie called from the driver's seat.

"Park and Fortieth. The 1600 building."

I looked over at Dane when he was done telling the cabbie where he lived. "Would you mind if I got dropped off first? I'm right around the corner."

"You're coming to my place. I don't want you to be alone after that little episode back there, and I thought it would be rude to invite myself over to your place. So, my place it is."

I didn't question his logic. It was sound, but still unnerving to an extent. I felt like a complete crazy person living a ridiculous out-of-body experience. I craved having my old life back, to be in the studio, behind my kit, with the other women of my band. That would never happen again. They all knew about my plot, playing into my freak accident and doing interviews on how crazy and tragic my untimely death had been. They all got it and respected it, and they'd moved on faster than I had been prepared for. But that's life: it goes on without you while you're hiding and scared.

Walking into Dane's apartment, I couldn't focus on anything other than how clean it was. Most of the guys I knew, especially musicians, lived like complete pigs—dirty laundry everywhere, dishes stacked a mile high in the sink, wouldn't know how to turn a vacuum on to save their lives. Dane's place was spotless.

"Make yourself comfortable. Want something to drink?"

Taking my seat on his soft black leather sofa and wrapping my legs under me, I called into the kitchen, "Do you have tea by any chance?"

Without replying, Dane started the microwave, and within a few minutes, I was holding a steaming cup of passion fruit green tea and sitting right up next to Dane. He put his arm around me and pulled me toward the crook of his shoulder.

"Just relax, Fae. We'll watch some stupid show on TV and you can decide if you want to talk about what happened at the bar."

"I don't think I can talk about it," I whispered, defeated.

"I understand."

Well, this night turned into a fucked up mess.

He flipped through the channels for a while until he found some sappy romantic comedy. "Here. This is what you people like to watch, isn't it?"

"You people? You mean the ones with vaginas? Yes. We do, for the most part, enjoy comical happily ever afters." I laughed and slurped my tea as he smiled down at me with that killer grin that was threatening to set my entire world on fire.

Damn him for being a smoking hot drummer with a smile that made me weak at the knees and gorgeous gray eyes that could pierce my soul.

DANE

I let Fallon doze off while holding the half-empty mug of tea in her hand. After I knew she was out, I carried her into my room and put her to bed. I thought about climbing in next to her, but that seemed like the wrong move.

Let's try to not be a total creeper the first night you're alone with her.

I grabbed a pillow and blanket from the closet and hoofed it back out into the living room to make the couch up for the night.

After grabbing a beer out of the fridge and finding something to watch that would restore my man card, I couldn't help but glance over to my cracked bedroom door, worried about Fallon. I knew she must have been pretty messed up from her old life, but to freaking pass out from hearing her old band's music at an open mic night was pretty ridiculous.

Fuck, she's beautifully broken.

It hit me. That's exactly what she was.

I heard my phone vibrating on the coffee table and winced at the name on the screen: Whitney.

I hit the fuck-you button and texted her instead.

> **Me: About to pass out**

> **Whitney: Want some company?**

> **Me: Not a good idea**

I knew if I didn't shoot Whitney down completely, she'd end up showing up at my door and freaking out when she figured out that there was another girl in my bed. Then it'd be worse when she found out that it was our new boss.

That would be messy.

> **Whitney: Are you trying to make me jealous?**

> **Me: Not in any way, shape, or form should you ever be jealous. Remember: we're not together.**

> **Whitney: Not yet**

> **Me: Don't you think if I wanted to the buy the cow I wouldn't have taken the milk for free without a second thought?**

> **Whitney: You just don't know what you want**

> **Me: I know I want you to leave me alone and let me go to sleep**

> **Whitney: Fine. Night jerkface**

I didn't feel the need to answer. She'd call me back in a few days and either we would have a very similar conversation or I'd give in to my smaller head and let her come over against my better judgment.

I set my alarm for an hour earlier than usual and let myself doze off.

CHAPTER SEVEN

FOREIGN TERRITORY

FALLON

What the fuck?

My heart started racing as I rolled over in a bed I did not recognize. I jogged my memory back to sitting on Dane's couch and realized that he must have put me to bed the night before. I jumped up, straightened out my clothes, and started to tiptoe out of his bedroom door.

Right as my fingers gripped the front door's knob, Dane's phone started blaring a horrible nuclear alarm sound. He shot up, a coy sneer rolling across his lips while stretching.

"Trying to run out on me?"

I bit my lower lip and shrugged, knowing I had been caught, my fingers still gripping the cold metal handle. "I just didn't want to wake you up."

"A guy brings you home, makes you tea, watches a god awful movie just because you like it, and then sleeps on an bumpy couch just so you wouldn't be uncomfortable waking up next to him even, though it would be completely innocent, and you try to leave without even saying goodbye? Ugh! Rude!" He dramatically rolled his eyes at me, shoving up from the couch. "At least have breakfast with me."

"I have to go into the office."

"Don't worry. It's six in the freaking morning, I think I will have plenty of time to make you pancakes, take you back to your place to change, and have your butt behind your desk before Payton has his morning coffee."

I rubbed my hand over my shoulder, staring at my feet. "What are you doing?"

His brow creased as he started to walk into the kitchen. "Being a nice friend. Is that a bad thing?"

I followed him into the kitchen, taking a moment to watch his muscular back flex as he walked shirtless, his sweatpants hanging low on his hips. Even Dane's back was sexy, with perfect definition and a tattoo of two fireflies on his shoulder with the word 'remember' inked under them.

"I guess I just never had a guy want to be a *nice* friend in the way you're trying. Maybe you are Romeo."

The corners of his lips perked upward and small lines formed at the corners of Dane's gorgeous gray eyes while stirring pancake batter and folding in blueberries and banana slices. I grabbed the coffee from the open pantry and started to fiddle with his coffeemaker until it hummed to life.

"Why don't you leave this work to me and you hop in the shower?"

"Do I stink?" I playfully shoved him with my elbow as I pulled open a cupboard, hoping to find mugs.

He laughed. "Yes. Like cow piss." His words dripped with sarcasm as he gently shoved me toward his bedroom door. "Come on. I'm really trying this nice guy shit, for crying out loud. My gym shorts and tees are in the bottom drawer of my dresser. You can borrow some so you don't have to put your dirty clothes back on."

"Thanks."

Once the steam was billowing from the top of the shower, I slipped in and let my skin turn pink from the scalding water. The burn felt good, reminding me that I was still alive, that somehow, deep down, I was still me. Everything was all so confusing, so intimidating, that I felt like I actually was dead in a way and had come back to life somehow. I hated lying, especially to someone who was being so damn nice to me.

I scrubbed off the loathsome feelings and the scarred exterior, deciding that I was Fallon Dunbar no matter what. I just had to go by Fae to protect who I really was and wanted to be. A few minutes later I slowly turned the handles in the shower until the water stopped, grabbed the towel off the rack, and dried off.

There was no way I could come clean to Dane, but maybe I could be more *me*. Fingers crossed.

His room was simple. Dark wooden furniture, a deep, red quilted blanket on his bed, soft, gray sheets that matched his smoky eyes, and a few black and white pictures of mountains and lakes—very masculine, very chic. I slipped into the first pair of shorts and shirt I found in his drawer then stared into the mirror hanging over his dresser.

Deep breaths.

Keep calm.

Try to let him in a little.

Sitting at the table, sipping on coffee, eating delicious

pancakes with Dane—it felt far too natural. We chatted about nonsense at work and how good of a guitar player Maverick was. I found myself holding my breath a lot when I felt like a question about my freak episode from the night before was going to jump out at me, but Dane left it alone, never even mentioning it.

My eyes started to travel around his apartment, taking in more of it than I had the night before. There was an acoustic guitar hanging on the wall above a simple drum set, but what really caught my eye was the massive bookcase that took up most of the far wall of his living room.

"You've got some book collection over there." I gawked at its splendor.

"Yeah. I really love to read. I'm a hopeless romantic at heart, but don't tell anyone! I'd lose my cool rock star edge if that was leaked."

I made my way over to the shelves and started to run my fingers over countless books, from poetry and classics like *Romeo and Juliet* and *The Old Man and the Sea,* to books I was shocked he had on his shelf.

I spotted one of my all-time favorites and smiled when I saw two of them all the way up on the top corner. "A double problem, I take it?"

Dane walked up behind me, smiling as he quoted, "'The best things in life aren't easy. They are tough, they are painful, and they are raw.'"

And then I finished, "'That makes the arrival at the final destination that much sweeter.'"

Dane blushed a little. "I told you I was a hopeless romantic."

"Maybe a pitiful one," I teased, playfully rolling my eyes at him as I nudged him with my elbow. "I cannot believe that a hardcore rock drummer has <u>Loving Mr. Daniels</u> on his shelf."

"In my defense, it was my sister's favorite book. She made me read it."

I looked closer that the broken, worn out spine. "Yeah, maybe the first time. Did she twist your arm to reread it?"

He glanced over at the books, rubbing the back of his neck. "Ok, you caught me."

A locked stare that would have normally made me utterly uncomfortable pulled me in closer to Dane. I took a few seconds to study his features: the diamond tattoo just under his left eye, the gauges in his ears from years of body modification, the way that ink swirled out from the top of his shirt collar. Then I looked into his eyes. They were smoky, deep, and edgy with an unfamiliar softness to them that was lined with brokenness.

That's when I noticed a few picture frames on the shelf next to me. Maverick's huge smile was the first thing that caught my eye. He was standing by a frozen lake next to Dane, who was holding a little girl in his arms. The next picture took me aback: the silhouette of a young woman who looked to be very pregnant.

After putting two and two together, I couldn't help but blurt out, "Do you have a kid?"

Dane sighed as he looked at the pictures with me for a second, taking the one of the woman into a shaking hand. "No," he finally whispered. The pain in his face clouded the room while he gripped the dark frame. "This was my sister. She died before the baby was born." A tear rolled down his face.

I put my hand on his shoulder but words did not form. I wanted to know who the young girl in his arms in the other picture was. I wanted to ask about his sister, to know her name, but nothing came out.

He shrugged, putting the picture back in its spot before clearing his throat. "I guess we better get you back to your apartment to get ready for work."

I looked over to the clock on the shelf next to me and gasped. "Crap! It's already eight-thirty! Payton is going to kill me!"

DANE

I grabbed Fallon's hand and pulled her out my front door in a hurry, only slowing down to snatch up her purse and clothes from the day before. I hated thinking about Leilani and how beautiful my nephew would have been. I hated the guilt that wrapped my heart. I hated the detestation I felt for my mother. But there was a time and place for all of my feelings, and right then, I escaped in the moment with Fallon, which was liberating and soothing to my boiling emotions.

We jogged down the three flights of stairs to the parking level of my building. I knew I should have been focusing on getting her to work on time, but all I could think about was how much I wanted to know her, how badly I wanted to make her late to work so we could talk about books over coffee in my bed.

What the hell? When did I start to like getting to know girls?

Even though at heart I wanted to be a romantic and find that cliché one special someone, my hard exterior and the walls I had built up over the years made me revert to a more typical male reaction toward women. I generally didn't care about them at all. Most of the women I knew or had tried to get to know me and the rest of The

Hysterics didn't help my perception anyway. They were sluts, groupies, or whatever whorish word defined the women who just wanted to lick a little bit of fame from the tip of a rock star's dick. In my opinion, sluts get treated like sluts. If they wanted to be treated with respect, they should have a little self-respect first.

"This one." I nodded toward my car while digging the keys out of my pocket.

I opened Fallon's door and then ran over to my side. As I slid into the seat, I took in how appealing she looked in the passenger seat of my car, wearing my basketball shorts and Blackhawks shirt. Her hands ran over the leather of the seat as I let the engine rumble to life and backed out of the parking spot.

"What kind of car is this?" her sweet, soft voice cooed next to me.

A smile spread wide as I thought about my prized possession. "This is The Judge." My voice was smooth and silky, the same way my completely restored, matte black Pontiac Judge with candy apple red leather interior made me feel. She was gorgeous and I loved her.

I glanced over right as Fallon rolled her eyes.

"All right." She chuckled a little.

"What?" I grazed my fingers over her soft wrist, right where fresh skin met with ink, in between shifting as we came to a stoplight.

"I never understood boys and their cars, the allure of it all. They're nice. Your car is gorgeous. But the way you talk about 'The Judge', it's like you just had the best sex of your life; I don't get it."

I kept stealing glances at each of her curves, the ink that decorated her pale skin, the bright pink of her lips, the softness of her eyes as they turned down at the corners.

"So, where do you live exactly? I know it's close to work, but that's all I got to work with here."

"Oh shit!" she exclaimed while we crossed over Jefferson Avenue. "You just passed my building, actually!"

I did some fast maneuvering and slid The Judge smoothly into a spot right in front of her building. "I'll wait here and drive you into work." I smiled as she started to get out of the car.

"Dane, you don't—"

I held my hand out to cut her off. "See you in a second. Go change. I'm not taking no for answer."

FALLON

From the time Dane and I stepped into the office until just after lunch, I barely noticed time passing. I was a whirlwind of productivity until all of a sudden a sinking feeling hit the bottom of my stomach like a Mack truck. It took an hour and twenty minutes, two sessions of praying to the porcelain gods, and half a bottle of Tums to get me feeling halfway normal.

On my way back to my desk, I saw Payton as he rounded the corner. "Fae, I was just looking for you." My face must have matched my light green top because when he looked up from his pile of papers, he leaned in closer and whispered, "Are you feeling all right?"

I fixed my glasses that had been sliding down my nose, then took the papers out of his hand, knowing that he needed me to edit them. "Just a little queasy from the Thai I had for lunch. I'll have these back to you soon." Right then another wave came and there was no saving myself. I ducked and lunged for the nearest trash can and wanted to die right on the spot.

You just fucking blew chunks in front of the entire office and your boss. Way to go!

Payton picked the papers up from the floor next to my knees and patted my back. "Why don't you take the rest of the afternoon off? It's Friday. Think of it as a little break, you've been working yourself into a frenzy."

I clutched my turning stomach, begging for this to be the last of the episodes. "Thanks."

He handed me a box of tissues from off of the closest desk and I wanted to die again—it was Dane's desk. He mouthed "Are you ok?" over to me and I faked a smile as I nodded while clambering to my feet. Every eye in the office was on me, everyone peeking up over their cubical partitions to see their new boss hurl into a white plastic trash can like a shitfaced groupie backstage at an Aerosmith concert.

I hadn't made it two steps into my apartment before my phone chimed at me with a text. I slid it open and couldn't help but smile when I read the message.

Dane: I know the answer, but how're you feeling?

Me: Fine. Seriously. I vow to never order lunch at that Thai place on 5ᵗʰ ever again.

Dane: Alright. Well we never got to have our "real"

date.

> Me: Now whose fault is that, Romeo?

> Dane: Yours! You fainted when we were hanging out last night, remember we were supposed to go out after we hung out with the guys.

> Me: Alright. I'll take that one.

> Dane: Rain check?

> Me: Sure. Sounds like a plan.

> Dane: Tomorrow night. I know where you live now so good luck saying no.

> Me: Are you a serial killer?

> Dane: Do you think you would have made it through last night if I was?

> Me: Good point. You didn't deny it though...

> Dane: I am not a serial killer. Promise.

> Me: Ok. Good. See you tomorrow night, Romeo.

> Dane: It's a date.

After a hot shower, a bowl of Campbell's chicken noodle with the cute little star noodles that I had always loved whenever I was sick as a kid, and lying on my couch for a while watching a few episodes of True Life on MTV, I finally started to feel better. I checked my phone for the time and seeing that it was only seven thirty, I decided to call my best friend. Homesickness was not something that really happened to me. I was used to being on the road with Regicide Assisted, but missing my bandmates was something I wasn't equipped for, especially Starr, the bassist.

Starr had been my best friend since we were toddlers. Our

moms went to college together and raised us to be practically sisters.

I listened to the line ring a few times and then it went to her voicemail. "Hi, you've reached Starr. You know what to do at the beep. Have a killer day."

"Tag! You're it. Miss your face and I hope you're out spanking the butt of that hot roadie from last summer. Everything is good here. Met a guy. Call me. Love you, Starr."

I slipped under the covers and let myself doze off just enough to not care when my phone chimed on the desk with a text message. A few hours later I was woken up to the squawking of a duck—Starr's designated ringtone on my phone. I threw off the covers and leapt across the room.

"Starr!"

"Hey, slut!" she slurred. "Miss you, bestie! How're you?"

"Good, just sleeping. You know, like normal people do at five thirty in the morning on a Saturday."

"Pish. I'll sleep when I'm dead." She cackled into the receiver.

"Yeah. Well I felt dead today. Get this, I puked in front of my freaking boss!"

"Gross! Are you prego? Prego peoples do that, ya know." She started giggling at someone. "Jake, stop it, I'm on the fucking phone!" she yelled, trying to make my band's former head roadie stop trying to play tonsil hockey with her for a moment.

"I am not pregnant, Starr. You have to have sex to get pregnant."

She ignored my comment and jumped to her next topic without missing a beat. "I saw the slimeball today!"

"Ew. Where did you run into Rhodes?" Kenneth Rhodes, my ex-boyfriend. I had thought I loved him, and then I realized that I loved getting high with him. I kicked the habit and kicked the guy. Right then all of it came falling onto me like a ton of bricks. "Starr, I need to run. Not feeling great again. Talk soon?"

"Ok, Fal-uh. Ok, love you, bye!" With that the line went dead and I went to lie in bed for a sleepless night of worrying the crap out of myself.

CHAPTER EIGHT

POSITIVE

FALLON

Those three minutes felt like years while I sat on my toilet, panties around my ankles, praying—I'd never considered myself too religious, but I figured I needed all the help I could get. The egg timer I'd set on the counter buzzed, urging me to look over at the little white stick that was going to tell me my future. Right when I saw that stupid happy face mocking me, I got physically sick.

Great, I have many more months of this shit to look forward to.

Starr's comment from the night before had replayed in my head over and over all morning until I broke down and ran to the drugstore on the corner. Now, here I was wading in the muck of her drunk ass being right.

I could not believe that I'd just found out my entire life was going to be turned upside down again. Only a few months ago, I had moved away from the mess of my past, stupidly thinking I could get away from all of it and finally have a fresh start. Now I was going to have a constant reminder and it was growing inside my own belly.

I stomped my bare feet in a childlike tantrum in my bathroom—screaming, crying, and damning my rash decision of letting my ex come visit me for one last hurrah. What a joke that was now. I knew he was a deadbeat junkie that cared more about his daily fix, guitars, and tattoos than whether I was alive or dead. He would not even be able to remember this if I tried to call him; the cocaine swimming in his blood would push this terrible thought right into the 'never calling the bitch again' file in his brain. I've been there a few times before, only being contacted for booty calls at four in the morning.

Before I became the assistant editor of Raging Underground, I was a deadbeat musician just like my ex. I was the drummer in a punk band, partying too hard and not carrying about anything important. The last three months away from all that had been amazing, except for the weekend that Rhodes came with the rest of my stuff a little over a month ago. I needed someone to help me get the junk from my parents' house into my new apartment and he was the only person I could trust to not blow my cover. We worked out a deal and now I was neck deep in that terrible mistake.

Working with writers and creative geniuses had been so inspiring. I was writing again and making good connections, even some friends. For the first time in as long as I could remember, I was really happy. Now I stood with one night's passions carrying consequences that could threaten all my hard work.

I turned the shower on and was starting to take my pajamas off when my cell vibrated next to my toothbrush. Looking down, my heart sank again, remembering I had promised to go on a date with Dane. I opened the text from him.

Dane: Happy Saturday! I hope you're feeling better.

Me: Yeah, I'm alright. Thanks for checking in.

Dane: You're welcome. I'll pick you up at 7!

After a moment of hesitation, I responded, explaining that I was not feeling up to going out, using the good old time of the month excuse.

Climbing into the shower, I tried to convince myself that I'd done the right thing. There was no way I was going to be able to hide my new predicament from my sexy, sweet, amazing coworker. I blushed as I thought about the night I went to their show, when Dane kissed me for the first time and how comfortable he made me feel when I'd stayed the night at his apartment. I had made him agree to take me on a date, and here he was trying to hold up his end of the bargain and I was bailing. It felt fucking awful. Not to mention that I actually had started to form real feelings for Dane. I really wanted a friend right then, and I hated lying.

After scrubbing myself harder and longer than usual with my loofa, trying to get clean after how dirty I felt, I climbed out of the tub to see a missed call and voicemail from Dane. I pictured his sensual crooked smile and his brilliant smoky eyes as I listened to his soft, manly voice curl around his message: "There are no rain checks or excuses that will get you out of this one. Too bad for you, I know where you live, remember? See you at seven, if you don't want to go out, I'll bring the date to you. Wear sweats, don't put makeup on, and I'll bring the ice cream."

I couldn't help but giggle at how amazingly adorable his gesture was. I got excited with schoolgirl butterflies crashing around in my already fragile stomach. And there it came, the second bout of sickness for this morning. It wasn't even ten.

This is going to be a long pregnancy!

After my giggles and butterflies subsided, I called Dane

back. The warm tones of his voice sent goose bumps all over my body while we discussed our new plans for the night. After agreeing to let Dane handle the details and promising to let him into my apartment, we hung up and I did a happy dance around my room.

I need to get a handle on these mood swings.

One minute I was ready to crawl under my bed and hide from the world, and the next the world was full of rainbows and cotton candy colored unicorns.

My Saturday consisted of crying, cleaning, wallowing, and frantically trying to figure out a plan of action. The crying came in spurts as more of the reality settled and marinated in my brain. Being in my twenties and just starting my career was scary enough. On top of that, in about eight months I would not only be taking care of myself but another person. I had just learned how to be responsible enough to not eat ice cream for breakfast, for crying out loud.

While wallowing in my self-pity, I cleaned up from my messy habits. There were no longer clothes all over the floor of my room, the garbage cans were all emptied, the toilet and shower were scrubbed, and the floors were mopped. I even cleaned out my fridge and used some elbow grease on my kitchen counters.

A terrible sinking feeling came over me right around three in the afternoon when my mother's name appeared across my phone's screen. I was not sure if I was even stable enough to talk to her, but I knew it had been a few days since we had spoken and she must have been worried about me.

To ease her mind, I answered, determined to make the call short and sweet and to not mention her new title as a grandma.

"Hi, Mom." I started pacing around my living room.

"Honey! Finally! It's been days." Her voice had more worry behind it than normal.

"I've been busy."

"Payton isn't working you too hard, is he?"

"No. I love the job."

"Good! How's the weather?" Typical small talk with mom; she wasn't too deep of a person. I don't even think she would be able to remember my favorite color (Kelly green) or where I actually lived in Chicago.

"Fine, getting warmer."

"Well, honey, that's great."

"How're you?"

"Fine. We started a bridge club in the neighborhood. That's been entertaining."

"How sophisticated of you."

"Well, it's a nice pastime while Sam is off working all of the time." I felt bad. I knew my mom was lonely but I hadn't really been home since I was nineteen. She was used to not having me around anymore by now.

"Gotta run into the office to get some stuff done, love you."

"Love you, too, honey. Talk soon."

Click. Good—short and sweet. I sighed with relief and started to work on making the grout in my bathroom white again.

I jumped in the shower once more right at six to get ready for Dane's arrival. I figured putting in a little effort on my appearance was a good idea for a first date, even if it was as casual as sitting on my couch all night talking. Excitement and butterflies returned as I pulled on my comfortable jeans and a loose-fitting black V-neck. I straightened my hair and put a little makeup on to hide how puffy my eyes were from all my crying episodes throughout the day. As I put on the final touches of mascara, my doorbell rang—there went the flutters again, crashing around in my stomach.

Please, don't puke in front of him again!

DANE

Standing outside Fallon's door was making my nerves boil more than I had ever felt before. I still couldn't freaking figure out what was so different about her, but I knew she was something special. She was more than just hot, insanely talented, and completely mysterious; under it all there was something so much more.

Taking a deep breath, I forced myself back into my confidence.

Here goes nothing.

I pressed the doorbell and could hear it chime inside Fallon's apartment. Suddenly, Fallon was standing in the doorway, a slight hint of makeup and perfume making her glow in her own beautiful way. Her smile widened as I held up the bags of Chinese takeout, pints of rocky road, and a bottle of red wine.

"I had to take a guess on what you'd like, and hopefully I'm at least not too far off." I could feel my face turning hot and had to divert my gaze from her bouncing tits, which were about to pop out of her V-neck. She practically jumped into hugging me around my neck.

"Thanks for this! You're sweet and rocky road is my favorite!" She took the bags out of my hands and headed into the kitchen while I was still glued to her doorway like a crazy person.

A sigh of relief spread over me as I took in a deep whiff of the incredible scent that lingered in the space she had just left and made my way into her living room.

Her apartment was nothing like I had pictured. I was halfway expecting grunge posters on the walls, a drum set where the couch was, and it to smell more like a bar than lemon Pledge. Surprisingly, Fallon's apartment was well kept with nice leather and wooden furniture. The only touch of whimsy was the bright green and orange area rug under the coffee table. Even being so clean, there was something cozy about the space and that helped relax me more.

Come on, man, get a freaking grip! She's just a broad for crying out loud!

Fallon popped back into the room from the kitchen with two plates, one wine glass, and a water bottle, then sat Indian-style on the floor to divvy up the food.

I took the seat next to her, eyeing the water bottle on the table. "Am I not allowed to drink or something?" I joked, taking the water bottle and breaking the seal.

She grabbed it from me, smiling shy. "I told you I wasn't feeling well this morning..." She trailed off and broke eye contact with me before continuing, "I don't think I will be drinking for a while."

I took the bottle of wine and glass, getting up from the floor. "Well then we'll save this for when you're feeling better."

I walked into her kitchen and rummaged in the fridge for another bottle of water, turning around just in time to catch Fallon wiping her cheeks. I was taken aback a little. *Maybe I should have given her that rain check after all.*

"Hey, Fae." I paused halfway into the living room, rubbing the back of my neck, not sure what to say next. "Ugh, you want me to leave? I didn't mean to force this on you."

My eyes met hers. They were piercing with sadness, or

65

maybe loneliness, longing for something I couldn't put my finger on.

She clambered to her feet and got almost toe to toe with me before responding, taking my hand in hers very gently. "To be honest, I didn't want you to be here, I thought I wanted to be alone..." Stopping to search for words, she stared down at our hands. "But actually, I really don't want to be alone right now. If I promise not to cry, will you stay and not ask me what's wrong?"

All I could do was nod and then wrap her small frame in my arms. I had never wanted to run away and stay as still as possible all at once before, and the sensation was completely terrifying.

FALLON

As I stood in my living room, breathing in Dane's T-shirt and begging the tears to stop running down my cheeks, I couldn't help but be shocked he hadn't bolted yet. I was a complete basket case and could not understand how his arms were still wrapped around me. I knew that if he let go my legs might give out from my mind swimming through this terrible situation, that all of the energy was completely zapped from my body. I could feel my knees balking and my throat tightening while I clung to his blue T-shirt for dear life. It had all just started to be real to me, and the near future completely terrified me.

"Fae, I'm not going to pry, but can I help you get to the couch? You need to sit and relax a bit." His voice was low and sweet, with a slight hint of I-have-no-fucking-clue-what-to-do-right-now. I was lost for words and I stayed paralyzed, scared to move, scared that if I let go of the only source of comfort I had, it would vanish into thin air.

Bending down and lifting my chin to make sure he made eye contact with me, Dane whispered, "I promise, I will not leave your side until you kick me out." He half-assed a cute grin and I nodded through the sobs.

In one swift motion I was being whisked toward the couch in Dane's strong, tattooed arms. He put me down with my head in his lap and stroked my hair in silence. He fumbled through channels until he found some idiotic grownups-only cartoon with a dumbass dad strangling his smartass son. I chuckled a little at the stupidity of the show and was so thankful that Dane hadn't been completely freaked out by my reaction to something as simple as not drinking a glass of wine.

I know it's said that pregnant women are allowed one glass every now and then, but in my state I could not be trusted. If that burgundy liquid slid passed my lips once, I was sure to down the entire bottle in one fell swoop. Staying away from it completely was my only hope of not drowning this little problem away and I was not about to do something so selfish. My stomach churned as I thought about the irony of learning abstinence at this stage of the game, but I figured it was better late than never.

We watched the rest of the show, laughing at the stupidly funny comedy, Dane's fingers lacing in and out of my hair ever so gently, completely relaxing me. Once the ending credits started to play, I shoved up and sat Indian-style on the couch to look right at Dane, my knight in shining armor for the evening.

"Hey, thanks for not freaking out. I'm just going through a little quarter life crisis, I guess." My voice trailed off and I had to break eye contact; I wasn't sure how much information I was willing to offer or how much he was willing to listen to. Either way, this was not a good start to a first date, if that was what our evening could even be considered at that point.

"Look, Fae..." He made me look at him again—he was very keen on eye contact, which I really didn't mind because his deep gray eyes were easy to stare into. "I haven't had the best life either. I know people might have judged you in the past, but I won't. I promise."

My face became questioning and my mouth opened a little, ready to start talking, to ask about his choice in words. Instead I just shook my head, completely confused.

WHY WOULD HE SAY THAT? DOES HE KNOW?

Thankfully, Dane decided to be forthcoming and continued, "What's in a name? That which we call a rose by any other name would smell as sweet."

My entire body got hot. "What the fuck?" My skin was crawling and my voice was shaking along with my hands; I had no idea what to do.

This is bad.

"I know who you are, Fallon." For the first time Dane did not look at me and a feeling of shock and panic spread like wildfire, tingling down to my toes. Hearing my real name roll off his lips stung at my ears.

HOW DID MY COVER GET BLOWN?

"How long have you known? No wonder you wanted to hang out with me. All the shit that spread about my death..." I felt sick again, along with being completely and utterly exposed. I had come to Chicago to prove to myself that I was more than just some cokehead rock star. I wanted more for myself.

I could feel the dread gathering in the pit of my stomach.

This is not going to turn out well.

CHAPTER NINE

MEMORIES

DANE

I immediately threw my hands in the air. "Fallon, that is not what this is about!"

Her eyes bored through me as her skin turned pale and her eyes watered. "Get the fuck out!" she screamed as fire flashed in her eyes.

I got up from the couch to leave but then something made me stop. I didn't know if it was how broken she looked in that moment, the fact that I didn't want her to have the wrong idea about me, or the fact that I didn't give a fuck who she was. I did know I wanted to get to know her, the real her, the girl who was broken and scared of being herself.

"Didn't you hear me?" Her voice broke as tears started to stream down her cheeks even more.

I fought through her resistance and wrapped her tightly in

my arms while I pulled her up from the couch. "I heard you," I whispered as my lips brushed her soft black hair, "and I don't care. You're not upset because I figured out your secret. There's something else, and I am not leaving until you freaking tell me what is eating at you. We all have a past, Fallon. We also all have a present and a future. Let's focus on that little sliver of a goddamn silver lining."

I didn't wait for her response; I didn't care what she thought I wanted to hear. I needed her to feel how real this was for me, how desperate I was, how much I didn't want her to hide anymore. I crushed my lips to hers, and for a split second she let me kiss her, deeply and passionately while I gripped her to me as tightly as humanly possible.

Just as quickly Fallon shoved me away from her, falling onto the couch in a fit of tears and heaving.

"Please, talk to me." I sat next to her, not really knowing how else to comfort her than to stroke her hair and grab her hand.

Her deep green eyes had flecks of red and honey in them as she wiped away a few tears. "I don't know how to say it."

"Just spit it out. It doesn't have to be pretty with a fucking bow on it. As long as it's the truth, that's all that matters."

She nodded but nothing more than quiet sobs came out as she collapsed into my arms. For a few minutes we sat on the couch as I let her cry, not knowing what the hell to do. Finally she looked up at me with bloodshot eyes and snot running down from her nose. "Promise you won't freak out?"

"Promise." I handed her a tissue from the box on the coffee table so the boogers could go away and stop freaking me out.

"Alright." She breathed deeply after blowing her nose a few times. "I'm fucking pregnant."

I gaped at her. Not because Fallon was pregnant, but because of the scene that flashed back and smacked me across my face.

"Hey, Leilani! What are you doing sneaking in so late?" My *little sister climbed quietly into my bedroom window because it was easier to get into than hers at three in the morning after seeing the boyfriend that she had been keeping secret—even from me—for months.*

"I just..." Her voice cracked through tears, but she was smiling.

"What's up?" I patted the bed next to me and she crawled under the covers.

"Promise you won't freak out?"

I propped myself up on my elbow. "I swear!"

She rolled over, grabbed her bag from the nightstand, and pulled out the white stick to show me. "I'm fucking pregnant!"

Leilani looked more freaked out and excited than I had ever seen her in my life. I didn't know what to do. I was happy I was going to be an uncle but I had figured it wouldn't happen for another ten years at least.

It took a second for me to cool my temper. First it flared red hot in my stomach, but I needed to be a good big brother and be supportive. "Should I be mad?"

Leilani shook her head in rapid fire. "Not at all." She smiled wide as a tear rolled down her cheek.

"Are you finally going to tell me who the mystery guy is then so I can kick his ass or shake his hand, depending on if he steps up?"

"Don't worry, he won't be like dad!" She rolled her eyes and pulled a ring out from her bag. It was a simple opal stone set on a silver band, a totally cliché high school promise ring.

"Alright just tell me!"

FALLON

"Dane?" His eyes were glassed over and his lips parted a little in the middle.

Fuck! He's in shock, why the hell did I tell him?

"Yeah?" He ran his hand over his face. "Fuck! I'm sorry!"

Well, this got awkward fast.

Dane's eyes got wide. "I am here for you." He stated very matter-of-factly.

He wrapped me in his arms again while his sense of calm melted me. I had never heard those words from anyone. Yeah, my mom and stepdad were supportive for the most part, but from a distance. Most of my former friends would have been on their computer already looking up clinics to take care of my 'situation'.

"Why aren't you running for the hills right now?"

He shoved up from the couch and started to pace around the room. "Because you need a friend right now and there's only one other person in this room."

"Why are you such a nice guy? How the hell hasn't the underground swallowed you whole?"

He stopped mid-step and cocked his head to the side. "The underground?"

"That's what I always called the rock scene, 'the

underground'." I made finger quotes and laughed at how goofy I must have seemed to him. A smile spread on his face, even making his eyes sparkle a little.

"What?" I had no idea what could have made him smile in this situation.

He shrugged. "You laughed a little."

Dane took his seat next to me and pulled me into his strong chest. "Look, Fallon. This whole situation doesn't have to suck as badly as you may think it will."

"Easy for you to say. You don't have to be connected to a slimeball for the rest of your life."

"Who's the father?"

"My ex."

"And that is...?" Dane's eyebrow rose at me while I stared at him with my chin on his shoulder.

"Ugh. Kenneth freaking Rhodes," I mumbled, feeling dirty just saying his name. Kenneth Rhodes had never treated me well and I could finally see it. It was liberating to know he was no good, but stifling to know I would have to do the right thing and let him choose to be a dad or not to our child.

Dane pulled back a little and had the exact reaction I was expecting. He fucking freaked like a stupid fan. *Doesn't he know that damn Kenneth Rhodes was the scum of the earth that just so happened to have more musical talent in his pinkie toe than most could ever dream of?*

"Like, the front man for Lithium? *The* Kenne—"

I cut Dane off, "Yes. And he's a fucking junkie who takes the stereotypical role of being a musician way too seriously."

He just sat there with his mouth open, staring at the blank

73

TV screen before muttering, "Fucking Kenneth Rhodes. I used to worship him, but I'll hate him if you tell me to."

"You don't even know him, you don't have to hate him. As person, he is terrible. As a musician, he's a damn savant."

"Are you—" Dane paused for a second, an unreadable expression on his face. His eyes looked so soft and calm but the way he was biting his bottom lip, I knew he was trying to choose his words very carefully.

"Don't worry, Dane. You can ask me anything, I think we have stepped into a no filter conversation."

He nodded. "Alright. Here it goes." He took a deep breath and then spit the words out, "Are you clean?"

It took me a few seconds to understand what he was getting at. I pulled my hair up into a bun to hide that my hands were shaking because of how nervous that question made me.

"Yes," I mumbled. I was proud of how far I had come, but there had been that one night all the shit hit the fan. Rehab hadn't been easy; giving in six weeks ago to half a Xanax, some ecstasy, and a bottle of tequila definitely was not a good move, and it had brought me to where I was now. That was the last night Kenneth and I were together, and the last night I ever used.

"Come on, Fallon, a little won't kill you!"

"Rhodes, don't you get it? I said no!" I crossed my arms over my chest and turned my head away from Kenneth's pleading eyes. "I just got out of rehab less than two months ago." I knew I sounded whiny and childish, but I couldn't help it. All of me wanted to give in, but I knew better. For the first time in my life, I knew how to say no and had the courage to.

"Just one last hurrah, babe."

74

Kenneth grazed the top of my hand with his calloused fingers. His steamy blue eyes were lustful as he licked his lips and let his fingers trail over my knee and up my thigh, playing with the hem of my short, white mini skirt.

I shoved up from the couch to stand over the table that Kenneth was kneeling in front of and stared at the crushed up white pill on my brand new coffee table like it was the devil. It called to me like a bad dream that I couldn't shake. It was alluring and majestic and scary. Then, as I had a million times before, I gave in. It wasn't even that I really wanted the drugs, nor was the booze affecting my judgment too much yet. It was that I wanted to give in to him. Just one last time, I wanted to be in that world again.

The next thing I knew I was on my back, smiling up at my rock god ex-boyfriend while he tied my wrists to one side of my bedpost.

"Tighter, Rhodes. They're not tight enough," I growled in his ear as his hot breath panted against my bare chest. He groaned at my words and did as I asked, cinching the scarf tighter around my small wrists.

His lips were hot as they connected with my neck. "You're so fucking hot." His words slurred while his hardness pressed onto my throbbing clit. He bit down hard onto my shoulder as he shoved into me. Hard, fast, no passion. He groaned as my hips bucked as he slammed into my g-spot. My climax built fast from the drugs and alcohol, making every sensation feel like sheer magic and ecstasy, the drug's name fitting the feelings perfectly.

CHAPTER TEN

REALITY BITES – FIVE DAYS LATER

DANE

I had to take a few deep breaths before knocking on Fallon's office door. "Are you ready?"

She looked like a wreck—hair in a messy bun, eyes puffy from lack of sleep from worry and morning sickness, barely any makeup—but she was still striking. Her warm smile met me as I entered the small office.

"Yes," she whispered, stacking a few pages next to her computer monitor. "Thanks again for this."

I shrugged, trying to play off how stunned I was by her simple raw beauty. "It's nothing, really."

We made our way down to my car. Fallon slowly ran her hand over the smooth paint, turning to look at me slowly before I grabbed the door handle to help her into The Judge. "Dane?"

"Yeah?" I grabbed her shaking hand as tears welled up in her eyes.

"I'm scared."

I nodded. "I know."

Wrapping my arms tightly around her waist, I squeezed her to me. "I don't know what's going to happen."

"I'll be there every step of the way." I kissed the top of her head lightly, reaching behind her to open the door.

She slid into the passenger seat and I slammed the door behind her. I was probably way more nervous than I should have been about this doctor's appointment, but I really couldn't let her know that.

Walking into the obstetrician's office was all too surreal. The walls were a pale pink with typical speckled gray tile. There were parenting magazines all around and random pictures of parents smiling adoringly at their newborns. All of it was unsettling, almost creepy.

"I'll wait over here." I pointed to an empty row of chairs while Fallon walked up to the check-in window. I glanced around the room at the few other people waiting. There was a lady who looked like she was about to pop and a couple sitting in the corner across from me. The guy was holding his wife in his arms while she cried softly and he whispered what I assumed were words of kindness and calm to her. There was also a mom nursing her baby under a blanket close to where Fallon was talking to a nurse.

It only took one level of Angry Birds for Fallon to come back with a clipboard of paperwork to fill out. I couldn't help but notice her hand shaking just a little as she filled in the different boxes or the tear that rolled down her cheek when she checked the box that asked about the current pregnancy.

"I'll bring those up." I grabbed the clipboard out of Fallon's hand when I noticed she had finished but was just staring blankly at the page.

I rang the bell next to the window and waited for the nurse to slide the frosted glass to the side. The corners of her mouth twitched upward as she took the paperwork from me. "Well, aren't you a sweetheart. We'll be calling your wife up shortly."

The comment jarred me a little but I didn't feel the need to correct her. "Thank you," I muttered before making my way back over to Fallon.

"Is it normal to be this nervous?"

"Yes, of course." I took her hand in mine, drawing small circles in her palm with my thumb. "You really have nothing to be worried about. I'm here to help you with whatever you need."

"Why?" Her eyes narrowed and her lips parted a little.

"Because you deserve it."

"There's more. There's something else. What is it? Is this about your sister?"

All I could do was close my eyes and nod. Talking about it was too painful; thinking about my family being ripped away from me in one moment had almost killed me once, and speaking about the accident would threaten all the progress I had made.

"Miss Dunbar?" A soft voice broke through the nightmare playing in my mind.

"Yes." Fallon gathered her purse, her sweater, and the pamphlets she had collected from the coffee table in front of us.

"We're ready for you." The lady waved her over to the door to the rooms; Fallon turned back and glanced at me before frowning and turning back to the nurse.

"The father is welcome to come along." The nurse pursed her

lips while keeping a warm, cheery look on her face.

I stood and walked over, putting my hand on Fallon's shoulder. "I'd be more than happy to come back there with you."

Staring down at her shoes, she put her hand on mine. "That'd be great."

I waited while they drew blood, talked to her about the intimate details of her missed period, discussed the last time she had sex, and did a timeline of how far along the baby was. Finally they ushered us into a private room.

"The doctor will be in shortly. Make yourselves comfortable." Handing Fallon a cloth hospital gown and a folded papery sheet, the nurse instructed, "Put the gown on, open to the front, and drape this over your lap. The doctor will need to do a pelvic exam before the intrauterine ultrasound." The nurse shut the door quietly, leaving us in stale awkwardness.

"Dunbar?" The sound of the nurse calling Fallon's real last name rang over and over in my head.

"Yeah. I am legally still Fallon Dunbar, so I have to fill out medical crap with my real name."

"Ah." I slouched into the rolling chair in the corner, not knowing what else to do.

FALLON

"Well, this is mortifying." I couldn't believe that I hadn't thought about this before I had Dane come into the room with me. Of course the doctor would have to do an exam, and of course I was going to have to get naked in front of him, and not in a good way.

"Do you want me to go back to the waiting room?"

Dane sat in the corner, barely looking at me. I knew there was something on his mind and this was a really hard situation for him too, but for much different reasons. I wished I knew the story; I wished I really knew Dane. He was like a mysterious rock star angel that had been sent for me just in the nick of time.

"No, stay. Even though this isn't how I pictured you seeing me naked for the first time, it's nice to have the company. Besides, the nurse who was taking my vitals in the hall said that we'd be able to see the heartbeat today. I don't think I can go through that alone."

He walked up and kissed me on the forehead while wrapping his strong, tattooed arms around me. "You pictured yourself undressing for me already?" He laughed a little as he spoke, lightening the mood, which I appreciated a lot.

I nodded into his chest before reaching up and kissing his soft lips briefly.

"I'll turn around, you let me know when you're covered up, and then I'll sit right next to you."

The thin gown draped over my shoulders, barely covering my boobs as I lay on the table feeling completely exposed, just waiting for the freaking doctor. Dane wheeled over next to me and gripped my hand.

"Are you at least a little excited?" he whispered before brushing the back of my hand with his lips.

I nodded as a smile and a tear slid down my face. "I really am excited. Scared shitless that I'll screw this kid's life up, but really excited to try to be the best mom I can be."

Dane's eyes softened at the corners as he pursed his lips into a small smile. "I think you're going to be an amazing mom, Fallon."

There was a small tap on the door as a blue-haired woman came through; I couldn't really believe my eyes. Most of the time when people refer to 'blue hair' they mean gray and old age, but my doctor was only a few years older than me with bright, electric, actual blue hair in one of the cutest short bobs I had ever seen. She had dark olive skin and piercing ice blue eyes. She was only a few inches taller than me, the perfect mix of fit and curvy. She was way too hot to be a doctor; she looked more like a freaking model or a front woman for a band. And then it hit me: she was the lead singer of a band I had met a few years back while in Buffalo doing a charity tribute concert for John Lennon's birthday.

"Molly? From Wicked Cadence?" My eyes were wide as I took in her features and tried not to sound completely baffled.

She blushed. "Have we met?" She stared down at my chart and her eyes got wide. "What the hell?"

I nodded, "Feel like you've seen a ghost?" I tried to not chuckle, failing miserably.

"Well, your secret is safe with me. We all have a past, just look at me!" She motioned to the name stitched into her white coat.

"I had no idea you were a freaking doctor!"

"Yeah, after medical school and all the residency bullshit, I thought music was my true calling. Needless to say, I was wrong. The band is doing well. Silvia Roland took my spot."

"That's great." It was nice to see someone I knew from my old life coming out of the shadows and succeeding. It gave me hope.

Dane cleared his throat. "Oh, sorry. Molly, this is Dane."

She leaned over me to shake his hand. "You're one lucky son

of a bitch to be having a kid with this chick. She's as badass as they come." We all laughed a little. "Well, I am sure dad is really excited to see baby's first photo, so let's get to it, shall we?"

"Sure," I choked out nervously. It was making me overly comfortable and uncomfortable at the same time that Dane was fitting into his part so well, and that I enjoyed him playing house with me for the afternoon so much.

The monitor started to show black, gray, and white, until a lima bean-looking orb was visible.

"That's the baby. Just about six weeks." The smile slowly started to fade from Molly's face as she continued to move the wand around.

"Is everything ok?" Dane's voice was low and shaky as he squeezed my hand.

"Fallon, I can't find the heartbeat."

I felt the air being ripped from my lungs and bile creeping up my throat while my eyes watered from the deep pain of it all. A baby that I wasn't sure I wanted was dead inside me. The sheer depth of my feelings of selfishness and uncontrollable vulnerability destroyed me on the spot. I shook and screamed out while Molly offered her condolences and Dane rocked me in his arms. I was no longer present; I was falling faster and faster down a rabbit hole of self-loathing and distress.

Molly's voice broke into my mind, "Fallon, this is much more typical than you realize. You did nothing wrong."

"How can you say that? There's a dead baby inside me!"

"Yes, sweetheart, I know. But your body is already starting to show signs of a miscarriage. This will pass like a heavy period, and in the next couple of months, you'll be able to try again if you want."

She handed me a pamphlet on early pregnancy miscarriage and her card with a number scribbled on it. "This is my cell number. Please call me if you need anything."

I took the papers and watched her walk out of the room.

CHAPTER ELEVEN

MENDING – JUST ABOUT 3 WEEKS LATER

DANE

"Just say yes, Juliet," I whispered as I walked up behind Fallon as she stood in front of the broken copy machine, about to kick it again and muttering obscenities under her breath.

She turned with an eyebrow raised and tired eyes. "What?"

"You're the one who called me Romeo first. But will you come tonight?"

"Dane, I told you, I don't know." Her weight shifted as a small smile pulled on her lips.

"But, you want to?"

She nodded. "Yeah, but I don't know if I am up for it."

I grabbed her hand, squeezing gently. "Let me take you out, get your mind off all this bullshit."

She sighed, staring at our interlocked fingers, but stayed quiet.

"Look, I have a surprise for you. You've barely talked to me in weeks, ever since the doctor's appointment. I get it, you needed space and all that shit, but it's time for you to smile again. It'll just be us. Please?"

"I don't... I just don't think I can." She slowly bit her lip ring, grabbing the papers from the copy machine.

"What if I told you I've missed you?" I cringed at how honest those words were. I had never felt so drawn to a woman before; I hated how vulnerable it made me and how mushy I got when it came to her.

God, I sound like a freaking pussy!

"I just don't feel like going out, having to get dressed up, ya know?"

"Perfect!" I sounded way too enthusiastic. I took a deep breath. "This is one of those times when comfortable clothes are preferred. Trust me. This will be good for us both."

She shrugged. "Alright." She lightly squeezed my hand then started to walk back toward her office. "Thanks."

"For what?"

"For being my Romeo," she whispered as she walked away, shoving the pages she was holding into my hands and saying louder, "Oh, that'd be great, Dane! I really *would* love for you to fix the copier for me."

I laughed and she winked at me, then smiled. That smile killed me and sent me straight up to freaking cloud nine. I tried to fiddle with the dinosaur of a machine as it groaned and stuttered, but it refused to do anything but print squiggly black lines.

I paced my living room floor at least a hundred times while I waited for Fallon. She had refused my offer to pick her up and said that she would be at my place around seven. The clock was ticking closer and closer to seven fifteen, and I was starting to think it was more than likely she was going to stand me up than actually show.

I shouldn't have pushed her. What the hell am I thinking?

I sipped tea and continued to circle my coffee table while the cooking channel played white noise in the background of my racing thoughts.

Finally, a soft knock echoed through my apartment and I felt like I could exhale.

"You had me a little..." As I opened the door I realized that I wasn't opening it to the right woman.

"Were you expecting someone?" Whitney was standing in my doorway wearing a tight red cocktail dress, her long, blonde hair perfectly curled. She licked her luscious red lips as she stared me up and down, running her hand over my chest.

"What the fuck are you doing just showing up at my place?" The sight of her made my skin crawl. I thought I had been clear enough that our relationship—or lack thereof—was over. I didn't want a fuck buddy anymore. Well, at least not her as a fuck buddy.

She popped her hip out, crossing her arms over her large, perky chest and pursing her lips. "You've been ignoring my calls and texts and I've missed you." She tried to touch me again, but I stepped back.

"Let me in, we have some time to make up for." She leaned in and tried to kiss me, but I shoved her gently back right before Fallon's voice pierced my ears.

"Dane? Whitney? What the...?" And with that, Whitney slapped me and Fallon turned on her heels and started to walk back to the stairs.

I didn't care what Whitney thought or if her feelings were hurt. All I cared about was that Fallon might start to not trust me.

"Fallon, wait!" I called after her.

Turning slowly to me, she mouthed, "Her? Really?" Whitney was still standing in my open doorway but I didn't dare turn to look at her.

"I'm going to grab my coat and lock up. Then we're heading out, ok?" Fallon just stood there staring at me.

"No. I think you have a visitor who needs some...*attention*." Fallon nodded to Whitney and then kept on walking toward the stairs.

"No, actually, Whitney was just leaving, and forgetting my number and address along with it."

Whitney stomped by us. "Wait until Payton gets a whiff of this little HR nightmare!"

Fallon stepped in front of her, smiling, her eyes narrowed. "What are you going to say, my dear? That you think I'm sleeping with one of the staff? Newsflash, sweets, I'm not the one in stilettos getting rejected in this hallway. Have fun trying to play the he-said-she-said game with this one."

Whitney stared, catching flies, while Fallon just smiled and continued. "I'm not saying that you have anything to worry about, but you definitely do not have a leg to stand on with this. There is no rule in our office that staff members can't socialize outside of work. If you ever paid attention to anything you'd have realized that we encourage our staff to hang out and bounce ideas off of one another, it breeds better writing. You should leave now. Dane and I have some plans that you have rudely interrupted."

That was it. Whitney was gone, but not silent. Within seconds of the stairwell door slamming, my phone was vibrating with 'fuck you' texts.

Fallon shoved my shoulder as I powered down my phone. "So you and Whitney, huh?"

The back of my neck pricked with heat. "Old news that won't go away."

Fallon grabbed my hand and started for my open apartment door. "Well get your shit and lock up so we can get going."

"You're not mad?"

She stopped in the doorway, blocking me from entering. "I dated Kenneth Rhodes. I learned fast that jealousy only makes you bitter."

"You must be the perfect woman."

"Far from it, but I'll take the compliment."

FALLON

"So where are we going?" I stared out the window, completely turned upside down. The light raindrops hitting the window streaked down as I tried to read the street signs at the intersection we were turning at.

"It's a surprise, Juliet." Dane's face was stern as he looked up and down the street that had no open parking spots.

"Dang it," he muttered as he pulled around the back of a dingy-looking bar at the end of the street. "I know the owner here, he lets us park out back when there aren't spots in front of Vatican."

"Vatican?" I asked, while getting out of The Judge.

"In black ink my love may still shine bright," is all Dane offered up as an explanation as he grabbed my hand and opened the back door to a tiny kitchen that smelled like burnt, greasy cheeseburgers.

"Are you really quoting Shakespeare to me again? You are such a pathetic romantic."

We made our way through the kitchen as Dane said hi to the cooks, addressing each of them by name all the way to the front bar where Dane stopped to shake the hand of an older man standing behind the old cherry wood counter. Glancing around the narrow space, I realized I had been there before: we were at Mountain Breath.

The man's face lit up as he grabbed dirty beer mugs off the bar top and scooped up some dollar bills left by his last patrons. He must have been in his late fifties or even early sixties, more silver than black in his hair. The wrinkles under his eyes and around the corners of his mouth hinted at him having a lot more of them from smiling than from frowning, which is always a good sign. The back wall of the bar was covered with old black and white pictures of a smiling, happy family.

"Hey, Dane! Long time no see!"

"Hey, Mr. Steele." Dane blushed when he said the man's name, looking to me while it clicked in my head.

"Who's this pretty lady with you?"

"Hi, I am, uh, Fae." Tripping over my fake name was something I needed to get over. Dane's grip on my hand tightened slightly, as if he knew how hard it was for me to lie. "I work with Dane." I took Maverick's father's hand, looking into his dark brown eyes as they perked up with pride, beaming over at Dane like a proud father.

"You can call me Marty. The Mr. Steele shit is too formal." Dane looked away sheepishly like a child getting scolded. "Well, I hope Dane is planning on bringing you by this weekend for Lori's birthday!"

"Don't worry, I'll try to talk her into coming."

I leaned onto the bar, winking at Marty. "I'll be there. Thank you for inviting me."

Dane cleared his throat and grabbed my hand again. "Alright, well we have an appointment at Vatican so we'll see ya later, Pop." A small smile spread across Marty's face and it looked like he might tear up a bit.

"You take care of Fae, now. She seems like a keeper."

"It was very nice meeting you, Marty. Hopefully I'll be seeing you again soon."

He nodded at me and we made our way out the door and across the street to a storefront that had a huge neon sign that said 'tattoo' on it. I stopped dead in my tracks.

"What are we going into a tattoo shop for?"

He spun me around and pulled my chin up so I was looking into his beautiful gray eyes. "We're getting tattoos together tonight. We're both going to start a healing process with a few simple words."

"What?" I was speechless. I never had someone proactively try to get me better. Almost all the peer pressure I had experienced was detrimental to my wellbeing. It was one of the best moments of my life, to look into someone's eyes and know they genuinely cared about me. "And what words are we supposed to be getting?"

He kissed my cheek and pulled a folded piece of paper out of his pocket. "I already told you," he whispered, putting the page in my hand and opening the door to the shop.

I stared down at the Shakespeare quote, beautifully drawn on the page in two different scripts. One was bold and masculine and the other was gentle and feminine with a small heart. I couldn't bring my eyes up from the page while my feet moved through the doorway; I was captivated. I had so many questions, but words escaped me. All I could do was let the script burn into my heart, cauterizing my open wounds slowly and perfectly.

Hearing Dane's voice snapped me back to reality. "Hey, is Cruz here?"

The woman behind the front counter was tall, skinny, and completely covered in inked art, even on her scalp to the sides of her perfectly groomed bright purple mohawk. Her pierced lips curled into a smile. "Yeah. Dane and Fae, right?" she asked while looking down at a huge appointment book on the glass counter. "Cruz is all set up for you two. You guys can head back to his station, if you'd like."

We both smiled politely and I followed Dane into the back room of the shop. It was a typical tattoo shop, open with stations spaced around the room and decorated with tons of pictures of past clients, paintings done by the artists, and signs that cracked me up.

'Tipping makes it hurt less.'

'I'm the tattoo artist your mother warned you about.'

We were greeted by a short, overly tanned man who looked to be in his mid-forties. "Hey, Dane, you made it!"

"Yeah, sorry we're late. This is Fae, the chick I called about earlier."

I shook his hand while he asked, "So what's the plan for tonight?"

Dane took the paper out of my hand and gave it to Cruz. "We're going to get these. I want mine here." He pointed to the left of his chest, right over his heart. "And Fae?"

Dane and Cruz turned to me at once—this was all happening so fast. The reality of the situation settled in and I started to get nervous, a completely different sensation than what I usually felt when I got a new tattoo.

"I don't know, I haven't thought about it yet. Where should I get it?" I asked Dane and he turned bright red for a second while looking over my body. I knew he had seen most of my skin while we were in the doctor's office so he knew where I was and was not tatted already.

"How about your right ribcage, do you have anything there?"

I took a sharp, deep breath in, exhaling slowly. "Nope. Let's do this shit! I'm first!"

Cruz chuckled. "Alright, let me get these on tracing paper and we'll get the ball rolling. Dane, if you don't want to wait, I have a new chick working for me, she's sick! Want to give her a try? It'll be on the house."

"Man, you know how I feel about free tattoos."

"Yeah, but this one wont suck. Promise. Serena just needs to pay her dues a little here. Tip her and we'll call it even?"

Dane agreed and Cruz left us to go into his office to trace our designs.

"Did you draw those?"

Dane dug his hands into his pockets and nodded, "I've had that tattoo in mind for years. After I took you home from that appointment, I knew it was time to get it."

"Why?"

"Why now? Or why that tattoo?"

"Why that tattoo?"

"Because some things in life just hurt so much that you need to feel physical pain to start to heal from it."

"Are you ever going to explain it completely to me?"

He nodded. "I promise, just after." He twirled his finger, motioning to the shop, and we left it there.

"Dane? Come here for a second." Cruz popped his head out from his office a few feet away from us. "I have a question about lettering."

Dane kissed the side of my head and assured me, "I'll be right back, try to relax."

"I am relaxed."

"If shaking knees equals relaxed, then OK." He gave me a fleeting half smile that sent my heart racing as he jogged over to the slightly open door.

"In black ink my love may still shine bright," I mumbled under my breath while I waited for the guys to come back out.

DANE

"Cruz, they're awesome." I watched as the only tattoo artist I had ever gone to put a needle to my skin and slowly drew the words that were about to be inked on our bodies.

"Do you think the chick will like it?" Cruz held up some of the most beautiful cursive lettering I had ever seen, tailed by a small, simple heart.

"Yeah, it's perfect."

I started to walk toward the door of Cruz's office when his words stopped me. "It's a big step... getting a matching tat with a chick. She must be pretty special."

I turned to him and nodded swiftly. "You have no idea, man."

I joined Fallon where she stood in the middle of the silent shop, looking like a sheep about to head to slaughter. "You know you don't have to do this. I just—"

Fallon's finger went to my lips, silencing me. "I love this more than I can even begin to express. Thank you."

Her eyes were soft and sad while they stared into mine. I knew we both had so much we needed to overcome, but there was a sense of comfort and lack of loneliness when I was near Fallon that I hadn't known since my life had crashed down around me.

A small girl with almost white bleached hair came around the corner and popped into Cruz's office. I could hear her soft voice through the open door.

"You wanted to see me?" She sounded more like a middle-schooler than a grown woman.

"Yeah, you're going to tattoo this onto my friend's chest. He's standing out there. His name is Dane."

With that the she came back into the room and walked right up to us with an outstretched hand. "Hi, Dane?" I nodded while she grabbed my hand and continued, a huge forced grin plastered on her face. "I'm Serena, I'll be tattooing you."

"It's nice to meet you." I couldn't help but check out all of her tattoos, from the mermaid pinup on her forearm to the roses on her chest, down to the sunset beach scene covering her feet. Serena had on a loose-fitting white shirt and tight acid washed jeans. She was absolutely adorable with her bubblegum lipstick and matching eye shadow—totally a chick that I would try to take home. For a split second my mind tripped as it tried to figure out what other tattoos might be hiding on her covered skin, but then I looked to Fallon's raised eyebrow and realized her mouth was moving.

Shit, she's talking to me.

"Dane? Serena was asking you questions and you just froze."

"Sorry, I got distracted."

"Yeah, I bet you did." Fallon rolled her eyes and walked over to Cruz's station, talking to him about her tattoo. She pulled her shirt up over her head while Cruz moved the Japanese screen to cover Fallon while she took her bra off. Even her silhouette was striking, erasing any thought of Serena from my mind.

"So, Cruz said you wanted this on the left side of your chest?"

I nodded, not taking my eyes off the screen. Watching Cruz put the stencil on Fallon made my blood boil.

Man, is this jealousy? It fucking sucks.

"Like here?" Serena touched my pec, grazing her fingers along my muscle a little more seductively than could be deemed professional.

I nodded again and looked down at her biting her lip.

"Take your shirt off. Let's get this shit started."

Before I knew it, the stencil was on and I was lying on

Serena's table with a watermelon lollypop rolling around in my mouth.

"Ready?" She was hunched over me, putting on her latex gloves.

I nodded.

"You're not very chatty, are you?"

I cleared my throat as the buzzing of the needle and the stinging started. "No, I am. My mind is just somewhere else right now."

"Behind that curtain or in the gutter?" Her coy stare was alluring but sweet.

"The first. Or maybe both." I could feel my cheeks burning while my lips curled slowly as I thought about Fallon.

"She's cute." Serena was trying her best with small talk, but I hated talking during tattoos. I liked to zone out and be left to my thoughts instead of the pain.

I nodded.

"Do I know you from somewhere?"

Crap, she is not going to shut up.

"Um..." I pretended to think, but I would have noticed her before. Her tits were too perfect and her tattoos were too sexy. "I really don't think we've met. I would have remembered you."

Too flirty.

She dug a little deep with a pass and I cringed.

"You look so familiar."

"My buddy's dad owns the joint across the street. Maybe I've seen you there?"

"Oh, my god!" She screamed the highest pitched, shrillest screech I'd ever heard. Thankfully, she didn't have the needle near my skin because I jumped about ten feet in the air.

"What?" My heart was racing and it was definitely not from the pain.

"You're fucking Dane Pearson! Holy fucking *shit*!"

I nodded, completely wide-eyed. I had never met a chick who got so excited about my name before.

"I'm really glad my name makes you so...elated? I guess that's the word for this." I propped myself up on my right elbow and watched the red-faced tattoo artist hyperventilate for a second, breathe a few quick, deep breaths, and then look like she wanted to crawl under the table and die.

"You ok?" I finally choked out while trying my hardest not to bust out laughing at how ridiculous she was acting.

"Uh huh. I just can't fucking believe it!"

"Believe what?"

"That you're Dane Pearson from The Hysterics and I am fucking tattooing you!"

"You know my band?"

"Know it? I *love* your band!"

I chuckled a little, nervous to even ask, but I needed this tattoo to be over soon or my pain tolerance was going to dwindle down to nothing. "Do you think...?" I pointed to the gun in Serena's hand and raised an eyebrow.

"Oh yeah! Shit! Ok!"

She chugged a cup of water then gushed for a few more minutes about how she'd been following my band ever since we played a summer concert a little over a year before.

Finally she got back to work and Fallon made her way over to my side. The calm settled back into my chest as I grabbed her hand.

"How'd Cruz treat you?"

"After he got over the fact that I have a tattoo under my left boob, it went well."

Jealousy bubbled back up in the back of my throat while the sudden urge to gouge Cruz's eyes out with a dull spoon coursed through my mind.

"Can I see?"

She shook her head. "It's already wrapped."

Fallon leaned over my chest while Serena wiped. "Oh, Serena, it's breathtaking!"

"Thanks! I actually didn't get your name."

Fallon looked down at me and I winked at her while she choked out, "Fae, my name is Fae. It's nice to meet you. Take care of him, will ya? He's my ride."

She walked away after glaring deeply and smiling sweetly at Serena, a small but cunning warning of possession. Usually I hated when chicks acted like that but the fact that Fallon-freaking-Dunbar had just laid claim on me made the hair on the back of my neck perk up and my dick twitch.

Fuck, I need her.

"Hey, Fae!" I jumped a little when I heard Colt's voice call out from across the room.

"Hey, we're almost done." Serena pushed my shoulder down and got back to work. "Just finishing the last letter."

"Dane! That's sick!" Colt's deep voice boomed and he leaned onto the table to get a better look at the scrolling letters.

"Thanks, man. What are you doing here?"

"Marty. I went in to grab a beer and he ratted you out."

"Sorry, man. This one I needed to fly solo on."

"Solo, my ass. Fae is here."

"It's different."

"Yeah, whatev—" Colt locked eyes on Serena, his mouth open. I think he might have even been drooling a little.

"Colt, this is Serena."

Her eyes got wide as her gaze darted up to my bandmate. "Ha-hi." She stuttered as she wiped my chest way too hard for how tender the flesh was.

"Am I done?" I tapped on her gloved hand, which was still wiping tiny *painful* circles over 'love'.

"What? Yeah! All done! Wanna look?"

I popped off the table with Fallon and Colt by my side as I stared at letters that melded together to form a phrase that meant more to me than I could even admit to myself.

"Excuse me." I ducked into the bathroom. The cold water splashing on my face did nothing for my shaking nerves. Seeing the words finally on my body brought so much more flooding back to the surface than I had expected.

FALLON

Dane sort of stumbled over to the bathrooms and I was left to watch Colt and Serena make sickening googly eyes at each other.

At least she's not fawning over Dane anymore.

Serena was all over him, eating out of the palm of his hand. She seemed nice and all but drooling over musicians just never made sense to me. *Doesn't she know that they shit and fart just like normal guys?*

"Yeah, we have practice almost every day. Why don't you come tomorrow?" Colt was sitting on Serena's tattoo table, holding her between his legs, his hands resting right on her ass.

That escalated quickly.

"Oh, my god!" Her shrill was deafening. "I would fucking *love* that!"

Colt smiled and cocked his head to the side. "Fae, you should totally come too!"

"Come where?" Dane slowly walked back over to us, looking pale with his hands digging into his pockets.

"Colt invited Serena and me to your band's practice tomorrow." Serena popped up and started to clean and bandage up Dane's new tattoo.

"How're you feeling?" Her smile had faded as concern washed over her face.

"Oh fine. I'm a big boy, I can handle the pain."

I laughed. "I'm sure the toilet agrees." I was hoping to lighten the mood, but everyone just stared at each other until Dane cleared his throat.

"Colt, inviting chicks to our practice, huh?"

Sheepishly, Colt nodded.

"Rodney is going to flip his shit."

"He can suck it. He's too much of a prima donna, I'll take care of him."

"Alright. Fallon, you ready?"

I said my goodbyes to Colt and Serena then made my way over to Cruz. Hugging him, I thanked him for an amazing job.

Walking into the cool night air, I hugged my hoodie tighter to my sides, feeling the sting of tender skin under the fresh bandage. Dane wrapped his arm around me. "Wanna grab something to eat?"

I shook my head. "I think I've had all the excitement I can handle for one night."

His back stiffened a little as he dug his keys from his pocket. "Yeah, we should get these cleaned up soon anyway."

We walked through the bustling bar and out the back door virtually unnoticed. Sliding into the passenger seat, I breathed in the smell of worn leather and pine air freshener. The car rumbled to life as Dane took my hand, pressing his lips to the backs of my fingers. "I cannot wait to see that beautiful ink."

"Cruz did an amazing job." The weirdest flutters consumed me. I was getting nervous. An overwhelming sense of needing to be alone washed over me. "Dane?"

He looked over at me with a raised eyebrow, slowing down at a stop sign. "Yeah?"

"Don't take this the wrong way, ok?"

"Don't worry, I'll take you home." He squeezed my hand before shifting gears and speeding off toward my apartment.

CHAPTER TWELVE

SKELETONS

DANE

Walking in my door, opening a beer, and watching boring television was too mind-numbing and infuriating while my skin burned under its bandage. I checked my watch: only ten more minutes and then I could clean up my newest artwork.

I channel surfed until Jim Carrey's goofy smile was beaming from my screen right as his character was talking to the waitress at Medieval Times. "Dos thus have thou a mug of ale for me and me mate, for he hath been pitched in battle for a fortnight and has the king's thirst for the frosty brew dos thou might have for thus!" I cracked up for a good five minutes, all the way to a commercial, and then my mind wandered back to Fallon.

I couldn't stop thinking about her. So, against my better judgment, I gave in and grabbed my phone.

Me: You should have let me come up and help you take care of that beautiful new skin.

Within seconds she responded.

Fallon: I think I can handle it. This isn't my first rodeo, ya know.

I shoved off my couch to hop in the shower, grabbing the fragrance free soap out from under my bathroom sink.

Me: Maybe I'm the one that needs help. This one stings a lot.

The steam from the shower bellowed up from behind the curtain and I slid in, cringing a little when the hot water ran over the tender skin on my chest. Right then it rushed over me, sending chills down my back as the black ink clouded the water.

"Dane? You home?" Maverick's voice called up the stairs as I stepped out of the shower.

"Yeah, man. Up here!" I dried off as fast as I could and threw on a pair of basketball shorts as Maverick came into my room.

"Hey, man, what's up?" Maverick looked like he had seen a ghost, standing in the middle of my room with his hands gripping so tightly onto his hips that his knuckles were white.

"You haven't heard yet?"

"Heard what?"

Right then the doorbell rang. As I turned to head for the front door, Maverick put his hand on my shoulder. "Wait, it's better if you hear it from me." He shuddered, his eyes flicking to everywhere else in my room other than my gaze.

"Hear what? You're acting strange. Where's Leilani?"

His head fell while a tear rolled down his cheek.

I gripped both of his arms, my voice cracking. "Mav! Where the hell is my sister?"

My best friend's voice shook while he fell to his knees. "There was an accident."

I dried off, trying to get the assault of memories to die down. There was no easy way to live with loss, but living was step one. My cell started to buzz on the counter as I folded my towel to hang it back up.

"Hello?"

Fallon's sweet voice came from the other line. "Hey, Romeo, aren't you going to answer your door?"

I heard a soft knock on my front door as Fallon hung up. I pulled an old Hysterics shirt over my dripping head and jumped into a pair of jeans that were crumpled on my floor.

I opened the door and saw a sight for sore eyes. Even though it hadn't been more than an hour since I'd dropped Fallon off at her apartment, I needed the calmness that she brought to me.

"Well, this is a pleasant surprise," I whispered as I kissed her cheek before letting her into my apartment.

"You seemed distressed, like a wounded puppy. I came to play nurse." She giggled, holding up a bottle of wine and some tattoo cream.

She was wearing loose black sweatpants and a white long-sleeved cotton shirt. Her hair was up in a wet bun, no makeup on at all, and she was wearing her black-rimmed glasses. She probably thought she looked like a train wreck, but she had never been more beautiful to me. There was a lightness to her eyes, a calmness in her voice, a truth behind the happiness in her smile; it was magnificent.

"Dane?"

Shit, I was staring and zoning out—not a good combination!

"Yeah?" I grabbed the wine from her, nodding toward the

104

kitchen. She followed and I started to open the bottle of wine.

"I think it's time to finally talk about all the skeletons." She hopped up onto the counter, holding her wine glass for me to fill up.

"Getting right to the point, aren't you?"

She nodded and bit her lip. "I've never been great at beating around the bush."

"Yeah, me either."

Without thinking, I gripped the tops of her thighs, pressing her lips to mine. Slowly we started to move our lips together, awkwardly falling into a smooth rhythm that was catalyzing the heat between us. Claiming her lips, I crushed her body to mine as her fingers gripped at the back of my shirt.

I picked her up as she wrapped her long legs around my waist. I half carried, half stumbled her into my living room to lie down on the couch with her on top of me. Our lips locked while I knotted her hair in between my fingers.

"I just don't get you, Fallon." I twisted my fingers farther into her damp, messy locks, jerking her head back to make her look into my eyes.

"What is there to not get?" I watched her lick her lips as my bulge started to press uncomfortably against my zipper. Her tongue, those piercings, her lips—they were all mesmerizingly sexy.

"You're just too sweet for rock and roll."

She smirked and bit her lip softly. "Sweet?" she growled, gripping my zipper. "I'll show you how far from sweet I can be."

I unclasped her bra as she yanked my zipper open. We rapidly undressed each other while we kissed, nipped, and grabbed at one another. All the pent-up frustration and lust that had been building between us was finally at its boiling point.

Pulling my body slowly onto hers, I traced from her lips down her neck, lightly sinking my teeth into the soft flesh on her shoulder. The gentle moans that escaped her lips made my dick twitch and my heart pound.

Kissing down to her hard, sweet nipples, Fallon's fingers ran through my short hair. Her breath caught as I slowly sucked and licked her buds.

Continuing all the way to her belly button, I rested my chin on her stomach.

"What?" she giggled as she grabbed my head, trying to force me just a little farther south. A growl came from the back of my throat—it was incredibly hot how forceful she was.

"The chemistry between us will blow this place apart and make it better through the destruction."

Fallon stared at me for a few seconds, frozen in her lustful position, letting the words sink in. She knew I could see that she knew exactly what those words meant. I watched her swallow a lump in her throat while she nodded. "Yeah. Wreckage always looked better than clean cut." She winked and pulled on my shoulder. "Come here, Romeo. I need to kiss that wrecked, beautiful mouth of yours."

I reached up to her lips, pressing their softness to mine, pulling down her sweatpants at the same time. She moaned into my mouth as she slowly spread my lips, letting her tongue search mine. I slid off the couch, putting her legs on my shoulders. There was no way I could go another minute without tasting her.

"Dane," she cooed softly while I kissed the inside of her thighs.

Gripping my hair in one hand, she gently led me right where I wanted to go. My tongue moved over her pussy, taking in her sweetness. The way her body shook and bucked from my licking and sucking on her clit was intoxicating. I could barely stand it. Her knees pressed harder onto my shoulders as she cried out, "I'm going to fucking come!"

Her body flexed and pulsed as she reached her climax, moaning with delight. My heart raced, I was sweating, and I must have had the goofiest freaking grin plastered on my face because when I shoved up from my knees, Fallon was laughing. Straight up laughing.

"What?" My cheeks flamed as I helped her get dressed.

"That was fucking amazing." She was out of breath as she pulled me on top of her, wrapping her arms and legs around me. "I've never had a guy do that."

"Eat you out?" I was floored. *Yeah fucking right.*

She laughed and kissed me. "No, get me to come while doing it."

Well, right there was the biggest ego booster I could have ever asked for.

We shifted to sit up and sip our wine. "Don't worry, Romeo, I won't forget about you." She winked and chugged out of her glass.

FALLON

"Are you hungry?" Dane shifted on the couch in the dense, awkward air. I was a little taken aback by how forward he was and how fucking fantastic he was with his tongue.

I nodded as my stomach started to rumble. I grabbed the

tattoo cream off his coffee table, desperately needing relief from the burning that was starting to settle in. Dane took the bottle, put a little dab on his fingertip, and lifted my shirt.

His voice was honey coated while he rubbed gentle circles on my aching skin, cooling the fire. "I know this amazing place just down the block. Wanna give it a try?"

I pointed at myself, a disheveled mess. "Like this?" I laughed, "Yeah right, fuck that!"

He smirked at me, putting my shirt back down. "I knew you'd say that. I know the owner, we'll get a booth in the back right by the bathrooms and no one will be the wiser to our appearance. Give me a second."

Dane dipped into his room and emerged in an outfit that mirrored mine: a white long-sleeved cotton shirt and dark gray drawstring pants. He ran his fingers through his short hair, messing it up perfectly.

"I'm ready." He grabbed his sneakers and pulled them on, then grabbed two jackets from the coat closet next to the front door. "It's supposed to get chilly tonight. This one should fit you." He handed me a black zip-up hoodie that was three sizes too small for him.

"Whose is this?"

Dane just shook his head, grabbed his keys, and opened the door for me.

"Alrighty then." I followed Dane down to The Judge and slid into the opened car door that Dane shut behind me.

"Are you sure I am not totally underdressed for this place?"

Dane was busy rattling off a text to someone, not looking up to answer my question until the sent sound swooshed from his phone. "We're utterly underdressed, but I let the owner know I'm coming in and we have a table next to the bathrooms like I promised."

The server poured our wine and took our orders.

I sipped slowly from my glass. The full aroma of the Malbec was intoxicating. Adding in the low lighting and white tablecloths, I felt like I was on a real date for the first time in as long as I could remember.

"This is nice," I murmured as my eyes wandered around the room, across the dark wood beams on the ceiling, down to the rich cream marbling on the floor.

"Yeah, Mav used to work here in high school and we still know the owners. They're pretty nice." Dane was relaxed in his seat, leaning back and just gazing at me, a small smirk playing on his lips.

"So, Fallon, tell me about you."

I fiddled with the piece of bread on my plate and shrugged. "There's not a lot to know."

"That's a load of bull and you know it. Come on, something, anything. I just want to get to know you better."

Dane shifted in his seat across from me, waiting for me to start talking, but I had nothing. "Like, what do you want to know?"

"What about your mom and dad? Tell me about them."

"Oh, them. Well..." I felt backed into a weird corner. I knew I didn't have to tell Dane what was about to fall off my tongue, but I felt like it was time to talk about it with someone. As I spoke, my mind played the scenes in my head, like a movie reel forcing me to recount that awful day.

"Mom! He promised!"

Mom sat across from me at the dinner table, staring at the ten unlit candles on the purple and pink masterpiece of a birthday cake she had spent the better part of the afternoon baking and decorating.

"I know, sweetie, but I'm sure he just got a late call and will be on his way soon."

"Ugh!" I groaned, shoving away from the table. "Is it too much for me to ask that he be here when I make my wish?"

Mom got up from the table, grabbing my hand. "Let's get our coats, Fal. We'll go surprise him at the station like old times."

I raced to the coatrack next to the front door, and within a minute I was in the front seat of our minivan, grinning as we pulled out of the driveway. As we started to pass through the last stoplight before the police station, we saw the flashing lights of a roadblock. There were tons of officers pacing around, a fire truck, and a few ambulances.

"Stay here," Mom ordered as she pulled the van to the shoulder and started running toward the mob of first responders.

She ran into the arms of Sam, my father's partner, and then fell to her knees, head in her hands. Without even realizing what was happening around me, I ran to her side.

"Mom?" She looked up with tears already streaming as she started to scream. She pulled at my coat, wrapping me in her arms as she sobbed. A gurney passed by me with an EMT straddling my father's chest and performing CPR as they wheeled him to the ambulance.

"And that was it. The last time I ever saw my dad's face. On my tenth birthday."

I pushed my Caesar salad around the plate, avoiding the burning stare that I knew would be filled with pity. I hated pity; that shit was the worst.

"I'm sorry." Dane's hand found mine from across the table, and he slowly laced our fingers together. Those small words and his slight gesture gave more comfort than I had ever felt from anyone else, maybe because I knew that he understood what it truly meant to lose someone.

I leaned back in my seat, finally looking up at his beautifully smoky eyes. "It was a long time ago."

He nodded, pulling his lips together tightly. "I know. And I know that the pain never really goes away."

His voice was broken and his face displayed his pain.

"What about you, Dane? Tell me about you."

DANE

There I was, sitting across from the woman of my dreams after she had finally opened up to me, and I was fucking frozen. I knew I needed to start talking sooner or later but I didn't know where to start.

"My mom was a single mom too."

Fallon's face didn't change while she stared at me. She just waited for me to continue.

"My dad left us when I was three and my sister, Leilani, was barely a year old. He was sick of my mom's drug problems, and

111

instead of sticking around to help his family, he ran like a fucking coward."

My palms started to sweat while the anger that had festered in my gut for so long started to get the better of me.

Fallon's voice brought my attention back to the present before the bad memories could start attacking me again. "Where's your mom now?"

"Logan Correctional Center." My words were flat and callous as they stained the air. It was all too bittersweet that my mom was locked up. I hated her for what she had done and for the accident, but she was still my mom and I missed the sober version of her that was a great mother, even though those moments were so few and far between. The air felt thick as silence blanketed us. I couldn't find words to elaborate, and Fallon didn't start in on the normal bullshit of cliché condolences and prying questions.

"Well...let's move on then." Fallon cleared her throat, sat up straighter, and refilled our glasses with red liquid courage. "What was this family gathering that Maverick's father was talking about today?"

I had almost forgotten about the annual cookout that was coming up this weekend until Marty mentioned it earlier. "Maverick's family has a barbeque for his mom's birthday and you're more than welcome to join us."

Taking a sip from her glass, she licked a drop that rolled onto her bottom lip. I craved to taste her sweet lips again, and now that they were coated in the bold flavors of the wine, they were that much more tantalizing.

"I'd love to. That sounds so—normal." She glanced down at her hands, a small smile developing slowly as she formed her words. "I don't think I've been to a good old fashioned family barbeque in, well, ever."

"Then I am glad to help you pop that cherry." My cheeks flared as we both laughed at my little joke.

"About earlier…" I trailed off, hoping that she enjoyed it as much as I did and wanted to build on it. Fuck, I just wanted to lick her again, and so much more.

"You're pretty talented." She winked at me, reaching for my hand.

I sighed with relief as our server came back with our entrees. At the server's request, I cut into my rare steak and watched the red juices flow beautifully from the cool red center of the premium filet. My mouth watered as I nodded to the tall, skinny server. "Perfect." He left us to devour our meals in peace, and for the most part, we ate in complete silence. Not an awkward silence, but a hushed knowing and understanding.

Once our plates were practically licked clean, my fingers intertwined with Fallon's. "How was your salmon?"

She rubbed her full belly with her free hand and sighed. "Fucking fantastic."

The server popped back over. "Would you all care for some coffee or a slice of our famous cheesecake?"

I looked to Fallon but she shook her head. "No, thank you. I'm stuffed."

I handed the guy my credit card before he even pulled our bill out from his apron.

We strolled through the double doors of the restaurant and the temperature had dropped at least ten degrees from the time we had gone in. I pulled Fallon's shivering body closer to me. "My apartment is just a little over a block from here. Do you mind hoofing it? I don't want to risk driving."

I hated admitting it, but wine got me drunk faster than I wanted it to. There was no way I was going to get behind the wheel after having more than one glass. That lesson had been ingrained into my brain years ago. I should have freaking thought of that before heading to the restaurant, but thankfully Fallon didn't seem to care.

"I don't mind at all. It's a beautiful night."

CHAPTER THIRTEEN

WALLS

FALLON

The chilled night air nipped at my cheeks while we made our way to Dane's apartment building. The walk was silent, soaked in our cavernous thoughts. Dane's face had a weak layer of a five o'clock shadow that gently scratched at my forehead as I leaned into him to block the soft night squall that whipped through the air. His arm never moved from my shoulders, keeping my cold body close to his warmth.

I just don't get this. All of it was so weird to me: the way we just clicked, how comfortable I already was with him. It felt like we were two puzzle pieces that had been missing from each other's incomplete lives until now. I wasn't usually a trusting person. I had walls—fucking high ass walls—guarding my heart. I was terrified of losing someone I loved so much ever again. Dad was enough. That's why I liked Rhodes and only had fuck buddies, never real relationships, before him. If you don't get close enough, it doesn't hurt that bad when they leave.

Dane was different. It wasn't work, it wasn't uncomfortable; it was natural. I didn't need to be around him every second, but every fiber in my body buzzed with excitement when we were close. Whenever I wasn't with him, I wanted to be.

Flutters crashed around in my stomach when we got to the security door at Dane's building. I was freaking nervous as all get out, so naturally, I stopped dead in my tracks.

"Aren't you coming in?" Dane held the door with his foot, running his hands up and down my arms.

I nodded. "Yeah, of course."

Cold feet? Nerves? Ugh, I don't like this side of me.

The light in the tiny foyer flickered while we waited for the elevator. It was musty and drab, almost depressing. The light gray wallpaper was peeling at the corners and the tile was in desperate need of a good scrubbing. The elevator dinged and opened. I wasn't too thrilled to be stepping into the small space; I hated elevators, plain and simple. I was terrified of getting stuck in one, and this one seemed to be a death trap.

Dane put his arm out to hold the door and waited for me to get inside. I was frozen; there was no way in hell I was stepping foot into that dang rickety contraption.

"Can we take the stairs?" I wrapped my arms around my waist, staring into the old elevator with disdain.

"Um, sure. It's six flights though." Dane shrugged and headed for the entry to the stairwell. "Don't like elevators?" He grabbed my hand while holding the door for me. The light squeeze of pressure let my shoulders relax as I took the first couple of steps.

"It's healthier to take the stairs." I smiled, continuing to make my way up to Dane's apartment.

Huffing, Dane kept up a good pace next to me. "So, are you coming to our practice tomorrow?"

My sneakers squealed on each step while I thought about it. I wasn't sure it was a good idea. A sinking feeling attacked my stomach and my heart started to beat out of my chest.

Step, squeak.

Step, squeak.

Step, squeak.

"I don't know if I should."

Honest. To the point.

Dane shrugged. "I'd like it if you came. The guys don't know who you are. We can just say you want to get more of an inside view on how bands work for an editorial piece you're working on, or some bullshit like that."

"Yeah, ok. I'll come. I'm just a little nervous." I cringed a little, giving in to the look of excitement that spread like wildfire over Dane's face when the words fell off my lips. "It'll be nice to sit in for a change and not be the one working my ass off."

"I should be the nervous one. Fucking Fallon Dunbar, the drumming rock goddess, is going to be at my freaking practice."

He swiftly jogged the two steps to get right next to me where I was frozen from nerves. My tiny ego was doing cartwheels. *He thinks I'm a rock goddess? Really?* Crimson spread from the tip of my nose to my tingling fingers and toes as he softly kissed my lips.

"It's going to be great. Don't you miss music?"

With every single fiber of my being, every single second of every single breath I take. It's an ache that will never be fulfilled again.

I nodded and kissed him on the cheek before starting to climb the steps again.

We got to the sixth floor and made our way into Dane's warm apartment.

"Want something to drink?" Dane offered, taking the loaner jacket off my shoulders and hanging it back up. As he put it on the hanger, the inside tag caught my eye: it had 'Leilani' written on it in faded marker. It took me a second to snap my gaze from the jacket now hanging in the closet back to Dane.

"Sure. That fruity green tea?"

He smiled while making his way into the kitchen. "Coming right up."

I grabbed the guitar off the wall and sat onto the couch. Starr had taught me to play when we were in high school. She wanted me to be the frontwoman of our band, not the drummer. Luckily that was one of the only times I did not give in to my best friend.

"Come on, Fallon! Please?" Starr sat cross-legged on my bed, giving me the saddest puppy dog eyes she could muster.

"N–O! I said no. I get bad enough stage fright as it is behind my set; the last thing we need is the lead singer choking or passing out on stage like a fucking psycho!" I tapped my sticks onto my drum pad, working on my hand evenness; paradiddles were threatening to be the freaking death of me.

Left.

Right.

Left.

Left.

Right.

Left.

Right.

Right.

I kept mumbling the pattern under my breath over and over, listening way too carefully to the way my sticks tapped onto the leather pad on my floor.

"Just picture the audience in their underwear! Isn't that supposed to cure stage fright?" Starr was relentless; it was one of my favorite things about her. I shook my head again. That was that, I wasn't going to cave this time.

Starr pulled her lips together, narrowing her eyes at me. "Fine. I guess we need to start looking for a sick ass singer. Glass Eyed Fish won't be much of a band without one."

I rolled my eyes. "We're not going to name a freaking band some pussy ass name like Glass Eyed Fish, Starr. Come on!"

She sighed in frustration, shoving up from my bed. She picked up her bass, plugged it into the amp in the middle of my room, and started to thump out a bassline. Her long, freshly dyed pink hair whipped around while she swayed and bobbed to her beat. She looked like Sean Yseult on crack while jamming along to the music in her head.

I climbed behind the small set that was in the corner of my converted basement room where my stepfather banished me once my music became noise pollution in his home. Electricity coursed through my veins as the music flowed from our souls.

"Do you play?" Dane asked, setting my mug of tea in front of me on the coffee table.

I shook my head rapidly, coming back to reality from my jaunt down memory lane. "Ugh, yeah. Kind of." I ran my fingers slowly over the metal strings; missing Starr hit me hard in the gut.

"Do you?"

Dane nodded, sitting down next to me. "I can play a lot of instruments actually."

I smiled. "That's not surprising." It really wasn't. Most musicians I knew could play multiple things. There was always one to be mastered and the rest were to play and clear your mind.

Letting the guitar rest against the coffee table, I took my warm cup of tea and leaned into the crook of Dane's shoulder. His arm wrapped around my body slowly as he kissed my hair.

"Fallon?" Dane's voice was almost a whisper, his chin resting on the top of my head.

"Yeah?"

"You can say no to what I am about to ask you." He cleared his throat before continuing, "Will you spend the night?"

My palms started to sweat. I wanted to scream that I would and that nothing would make me happier, but for some reason I was scared shitless. It wasn't about staying in Dane's apartment—been there, done that. It wasn't even being scared of having sex with him. I'd wanted to ride in that rodeo ever since that first kiss of ours, and now that I knew how talented he was with his tongue, I could only image the amazing things he could do with other parts of his body. I was scared that he was starting to break down my walls more than I was prepared for, getting too close for me to ever be able to walk away from him.

Against my better judgment, I sighed and leaned more into him. "I'd love to."

DANE

After two cups of tea, my goofy ass trying to serenade Fallon, and her truly shocking me with how amazingly well she could sing, we made our way to my room. There was something so sweet and innocent about our evening and for the first time, I didn't want to have sex with the woman crawling into my bed wearing a pair of basketball shorts and my faded navy shirt that had the name of my band sprawled across her tits. I wanted to love her.

"What time do you need to be up?" Fallon's head was already resting on the pillow when she looked up at me, a soft, sleepy smile lingering on her gorgeously pierced lips.

"I need to be in the office at nine tomorrow, so seven?" She stretched while I climbed into bed next to her.

"Alright." I set the alarm on my phone, plugged it in, and hit the remote on my nightstand to turn the fan up and the light off.

I innocently kissed Fallon on the cheek, resting my head back down on my pillow. Soft kisses started brushing my bare shoulder and slowly worked their way up my neck with swift, gentle nibbles. The smooth metal of Fallon's lip rings ran over my skin, spreading chills over my shoulders. Her body shifted closer to mine. Her lips were soft but firm, innocent but seductive. They were like honey mixing with cayenne pepper, spreading a silky warmth that I had never felt before.

I moaned and flexed under her tender touch as her fingertips trailed up my abs. "We don't have to—" I muttered before she cut me off.

"Shhh...I said I was going to return the favor, Romeo." Her nails gently dug into the flesh over my hipbone as she crushed her lips to mine. Desire dripped into my mouth from hers and it was completely infectious. There was so much need behind her kiss as she hungrily moved my lips apart and explored my mouth with her tongue.

I forcefully pulled her on top of me, gripping her ass firmly in my hands. "Fuck..." I growled. I could feel my dick getting harder at the very thought of her enjoying our little foreplay; I couldn't image how amazing it was going to feel once I was actually inside her.

"I want you," she breathed while nibbling on my earlobe.

I tangled my fingers into her hair, ripping her head back sharply. "Let's get one thing straight: I'm a nice guy, but once we start, I'm rough and in charge and not *nice*." The words felt like gravel pouring off my tongue as I thirsted for her mouth again.

Fallon rolled her tongue over my bottom lip, biting it gently. "Good. I don't like sweet when it comes to this." She glanced down and back up, starting to fumble with the drawstring on my basketball shorts.

I pulled my shirt off of her, exposing her gorgeous tits, and slid my shorts down as fast as possible. In one fell swoop, Fallon was on her knees sucking my balls, my feet firmly planted on the floor as I gripped the pillow behind my head. Every tongue flick and tease of her teeth sent chills throughout my entire body. Her lip rings glided over my sensitive skin. *Holy fuck.* It felt incredible.

A deep rumble came from deep in my chest as I took her locks in between my fingers again and positioned her lips over the head of my pre-come soaked dick. She practically purred while she rubbed her fingers over the base of my shaft and sucked gently on the head. It was fucking ecstasy—pure ecstasy—having her gorgeous mouth feasting on me.

My shoulders tensed and my breath quickened, matching hers. I pulled her head back and made her lock eyes with me. "I want to fuck your pretty mouth so badly."

She smiled with hooded eyes. "Then do it."

It was almost a dare that I was more than willing to accept. She opened her mouth and I thrust my dick right into the back of her throat. She choked—hard. I pulled out and waited for her to bitch about me hurting her, but she licked the wetness from the tip of my dick. "Is that all?"

I smirked. *This is going to be a fun night.*

I pumped my cock in and out of her mouth as she took me deeper and deeper into her throat, her eyes watering slightly, but every time I'd hesitate she smiled and egged me on to continue.

"Damn it, Fallon, let me fuck you!" My voice was husky, filled with need.

"Where are the condoms?"

I pointed to the second drawer in my nightstand. She ripped the package open with her teeth, straddled my hips and rolled the latex over my cock slowly, biting her bottom lip while she watched my every reaction to her touch.

"God, you're so fucking sexy," I breathed, gripping her hips and sliding her slowly onto me.

She rolled her head back and moaned, taking my length in. "Your dick feels so good."

Fallon started to rock her hips and I followed suit, letting her set our pace while her lips curled into a seductive smirk. Her hands gripped onto my shoulders as her tits bounced only an inch from my chest. It was the most incredibly sexy sight I had ever seen in my life. Her gorgeous tattoos were hard to make out in the dim light, but I could see their faint beauty, along with her small curves and her perfect boobs. I was fucking mesmerized until she locked her lips onto mine and moaned from the back of her throat into me, "I'm about to fucking come."

That was my cue, and it was fucking perfect. We climaxed together, our bodies shuddering and twitching in unison.

My chest heaved as her head fell onto it.

"That was freaking incredible." Her lips dusted over my pec as she kissed my freshly tattooed skin gently.

Fallon walked into my bathroom, holding the shirt and shorts that she had borrowed. I grabbed a tissue from the nightstand, pulled the condom off, and cleaned my jizz-soaked cock. I grabbed a fresh pair of boxers out of drawer, still shaking a little, and climbed back into bed. Fallon came back, looking more stunning than ever. Right then it hit me: she was fucking mine. In that moment, I had claimed her. I had never felt that way before, but there it was, staring at me from the other side of my bed. Her eyes told the same story: she knew that I was hers too.

Fallon rolled on her side away from me. Her hair smelled so sweet and familiar, just like home. I wrapped her in my arms, nuzzling my nose into the loose hair that rested on her shoulder. I kissed her neck gently. "Goodnight."

She mumbled what I assumed was "Night" and we both drifted off into dreamland.

"No—Sam! Stop, please!" Fallon muttered and cried in her sleep as she thrashed about, tangling herself in my sheets.

I tried to shake her gently, but at my touch she took a swing.

Fallon was having a full-on night terror in my bed. I remembered Leilani getting them when she was really young and her doctors told us that as long as she wasn't hurting herself, it was better to let the terror play out. I turned on the light, staying on the other side of the bed and trying to make mental notes about everything she was blurting out. She just kept saying different combinations of the same words: "No, Sam, stop, please, you're hurting me."

She finally settled down after about a fifteen minute episode and I was able to fall back to sleep.

The alarm on my nightstand blared from my phone way earlier than I wanted it to. Groggily, I shook Fallon. "Hey, it's time to get up."

Grumble, grumble, grumble. That's all I could get out of her for about five minutes.

"Fallon, we can't be late to work." I whispered into her ear.

"Ugh! I feel like I barely slept." She yawned while rubbing her eyes.

I scooped her tired body into my arms. "Who's Sam?" I blurted out the question, scared shitless of the answer.

Her body got rigid as she pulled away to look at me. There was something in her eyes that I had never seen before, like fear mixed with something else I couldn't identify. "Sam is my stepfather's name. Why?"

I rubbed my hand over my face before answering, "You had a really bad nightmare last night. You kept saying stuff like, 'Sam stop,' and 'You're hurting me.'"

She swallowed hard as her skin turned pale. She shook her head fast. "It's nothing. I've been having bad dreams about him since I was a kid. I was mad that my mom married my dad's partner. I felt betrayed."

125

I couldn't help but feel like there was something there that Fallon wasn't admitting, even to herself, but leaving it alone seemed like the best thing for now. I kissed her soft hair and grabbed her hand. "Alright."

Her eyes filled with tears while she choked, "It's nothing really. He just had a heavy hand and a bad temper. As I grew up, he grew out of it."

I nodded. "My old man enjoyed belting me a little more than he should have before he ran out. Thankfully Leilani was too little for him to use corporal punishment on."

Fallon sat on my bed, pulling her sneakers back onto her feet in a deep silent thought, then looked up at me. "I'm going to make a pot of coffee and then we need to head out."

I nodded and that was that, sharing time was over. She was so reserved and closed off, but I wanted to break down the walls and really get to know who Fallon was. One thing was certain: I was just going to have to be patient.

CHAPTER FOURTEEN

PRACTICE

FALLON

Sitting in on Whitney's disciplinary meeting with Payton was very entertaining for me. I shouldn't have enjoyed watching her brow crease, her knee bounce uncontrollably, or her frown lines make her usually beautiful facial features retreat with fear and nerves, but she looked like a wreck and I loved it.

Payton sat at one end of the boardroom's large oval mahogany table with me to his left and Whitney sweating it out like crazy at the other end.

"Do you know why I called this meeting, Ms. Quints?"

I could see her swallow hard as she shook her head, directing her gaze at the tabletop.

"It has been apparent for some time now that your writing has been, what's the right word?" He looked at me to answer.

"Slacking?" I happily offered.

Payton nodded in agreement. "Yes. It seems like you've lost a bit of your mojo lately, my dear. Frankly, I'm concerned about you and your future at Raging Underground if this is the quality you continue to produce."

Payton handed me her latest article, which he had insisted on reviewing personally. As such, it was now a battlefield of pen marks attacking the pages. "I am going to have Fae review some of your older work and compare it to some of your more recent articles. Hopefully she will be able to give you some positive critiques on how to get your head back in the game. I strongly advise you listen to Ms. Dunham and take her advice to heart, Ms. Quints. Please sign this paper before you leave, it is a ninety day probation notice. That's how much time you will have to redeem yourself here."

I took the printouts of Whitney's writing and shoved them into a folder, then left Whitney to ask Payton questions in private if she wanted. Even though I enjoyed her not having the best of days, I wasn't a completely conniving bitch; I didn't want anyone to be fired.

The rest of my day seemed to zoom by. With having to deal with Whitney's slacking writing skills on top of all of the articles that needed to be polished for the next publication, I didn't even notice when most of the office was empty.

There was a soft knock on my office door and I looked up to see Payton smiling at me from the doorway.

"You're really doing a great job here, my dear." He walked in, taking a seat in the bright red armchair on the other side of my desk. "You remind me of him so much."

I closed my laptop screen, trying to muster a smile. "I wish I remembered more of him."

"Oh, my dear, he was a good man and he loved you and your mom so much. I remember when he called to tell me that you were born like it was yesterday. He always had a pretty tough exterior; that moment of pride and the happy tears I could hear in his voice were more raw and real than any emotion I had ever gotten from him."

A tear rolled down my cheek. "Thanks, Payton. I needed that."

He nodded. "I know." He winked and got up from his chair. "I know your mother's second marriage was hard on you. I should have stayed more involved in your life after Rick died. I'm just glad you're here now."

"Fate works in mysterious ways."

"You have no idea, Fallon. Go home. You've worked hard enough today."

I organized my desk, put my laptop into my briefcase, and was walking out of the double doors of the office building within ten minutes. As a cab pulled up to the curb, I got a text.

Dane: Are you still coming?

Me: Yeah, just leaving work now. I'm going to run home to change real quick.

Dane: Sounds good, Juliet.

Me: Is there anything you need me to bring? Beer, snacks? I really don't know how this is supposed to work.

Dane: You're too cute. Colt's mom has a loaded pantry and we have his old man's stash of PBR. Just get your cute ass here soon.

Me: Why the rush?

Dane: Colt's chick has been here for an hour and I am sick of him making googly eyes at her while she fangirls all

over this place, I need someone to ground me.

Me: I'm coming straight there.

I knew all too well how terrible it was when there were distractions during a practice, even if it was a hot piece of eye candy. Practice should be treated like any other job: with respect and focus. If you can't get with the program, get the fuck out.

"Can we actually go here?" I handed the cabbie the address Dane had scribbled onto a pink sticky note before he left the office a few hours before.

"Sure thing, sweets."

I paid the cabdriver and called Dane, smiling when I saw The Judge parked in the driveway as I exited the yellow cab.

"Hey." His voice sounded so husky.

Weak knees.

Stomach flutters.

With only one freaking word.

I had it bad. And that wasn't a bad thing at all. It was pretty exhilarating, even though I felt like butterflies were going to leap out of my stomach at any moment.

"Just pulled up."

"I'll be right there."

It only took Dane a few seconds before he was opening the door to Colt's family home. It was a two story brick house that looked so warm and inviting, even from the outside.

Dane beamed at me from the doorway as he leaned on the doorjamb, propping the door open with his foot. "Thanks for coming." He pecked me hastily on the lips. Even that quick, simple touch sent electricity through my body.

"Thanks for having me."

Dane's fingers weaved between mine as he led me down into the finished basement where everyone was, my heels clicking on the hardwood floors the whole way. I felt incredibly overdressed in my pencil skirt, button down blouse, and blazer. I also felt insanely uncomfortable; I wasn't usually one to dress like a lawyer. I preferred skinny jeans, band tees, and my worn in Chucks.

We descended into a typical man cave basement, any musician's wet dream come true. There were amps, guitars, state-of-the-art sound equipment, and two drum sets taking up most of the large space. A few folding chairs, a worn out couch, and a large fridge took up the rest of the room. The only items that seemed out of place were the washer and dryer tucked into the far corner under the stairs with folded clothes in a basket.

I hugged each one of the guys and told Colt how much I loved what I had seen of the house so far.

"Yeah, my mom is an interior designer. She'll be thrilled when I relay the compliment her way. You remember Serena, right?"

I smiled over to the fading rosy leather couch as Serena popped up and bounced over to me. "Of course I remember you!" I attempted to infuse some giddiness into my voice; it seemed flat and callous to me, but Serena seemed to buy it as she wrapped me in a hug.

"It's so great to see you again." Her soft, high-pitched voice was so innocent and childlike—it did not match her tatted exterior one bit. "How's the ink healing?"

I pulled up my blouse to show the forming scabs that itched like crazy. "It's doing great."

Dane handed me a beer, kissed me on the cheek, and turned to his bandmates. "Alright, gents, break time is fucking over."

Watching him climb behind his drum set sent flutters through my whole body. I was freaking nervous as all get out. I longed to be back there instead of him; I was stoked to hear them play more, but I itched to play again.

Calm your tits, Fallon. You're Fae fucking Dunham, remember?

"Eeek!" Serena's elation broke me from my thoughts.

I turned to her. "Huh?" I was totally dumbfounded by how utterly uncool she was being. Didn't she know that fawning over rock stars is the opposite of what is actually attractive?

She leaned in close so I could hear her over the booming of amps. "This is one of my favorites from their first album!"

"It is really awesome." I smiled at Dane as he winked at me. Enjoyment and pride dripped from him while he played away. Right then, that's when Dane was the most attractive to me. He was simply talented and confident, and fuck, it was so sexy.

"Can you *believe* they're letting *us* be here? This is freaking amazing! I am freaking out!"

"Yeah, it's pretty cool." I tried to sound as excited as she was, but I was failing. To be honest, my insides were doing cartwheels, and not in a good way—especially when I heard a missed opportunity in the hook of the song.

Keep your lips sealed.

I bit my tongue and clapped when the song was done. "That was great, guys."

Dane looked at me with a raised eyebrow. "I saw that frown in the middle."

Shit.

I shook my head while the band all glued their eyes on me.

Dane took a swig from his bottle of water as I gulped down half of my beer. "What did you hear, Fae?" Hearing him use my fake name felt so wrong. It was gross.

Maverick looked over at me. "Yeah, any advice is good."

"But you guys are the musicians, not me."

Maverick shot me a sweet smile while wiping his sweat-soaked brow. "We don't have outsiders in practice often. Sometimes others hear things we don't."

I bit my lip. My heart was pounding out of my chest.

"Alright, in the hook, there was a point where if you let the bottom fall out, the reentry would be really powerful."

They all looked at me like I had six heads.

"Ok, ok. What do I know? I'm just a journalist."

Dane laughed a little to himself and if looks could kill, the daggers shooting from my eyes would have had him sprawled out in two seconds flat.

Maverick looked at me, then to Dane with a knowing smile.

He can't know. Don't be ridiculous, Fallon—I mean Fae! Shit balls of fire!

"Try to explain it." Dane's husky voice floated over to me and I started to search through Spotify for the sound I was thinking of.

"Ok here." I skipped through Something Corporate's "I Want to Save You" until a little before the bridge. "Listen to the piano fall out and then rush back in, it's so freaking powerful."

Rodney looked like a light bulb had just exploded in his face. "That is fucking brilliant. Good ear, Fae. Maybe you should have been a musician." He winked at me and grabbed his mic, slinging his guitar strap back over his head.

His words bit at my cheeks as they flamed red. "Yeah, maybe." I shrugged, trying to calm my shaking nerves and voice. "Where's the restroom?"

I needed to get the fuck out of there for a little bit. I could feel the tears starting to sting the backs of my eyes and I did not want to look like a freaking nutcase in front of these guys. Serena was enough crazy for one evening.

"I'll show you." Maverick pointed up the stairs and started to lead the way.

Once the basement door was shut behind us, he turned to me. "Fallon, thank you for that advice." The feeling of his hand on my shoulder burned as the sound of my real name festered in the air.

"How'd you...?" I couldn't even get the words to come out of my throat.

"Does it matter?"

I shook my head and turned for the bathroom, slamming the basement door behind me. I splashed water on my face and stared blankly into my reflection in the mirror. I barely looked like my old self anymore: soft pink and neutral makeup, fake glasses, a collared white blouse under a dark blue blazer, French manicured nails. I missed the heavy makeup, the bright red lipstick, the black nail polish, my rocker edge and confidence. It was replaced by a nervous girl who was scared of her own shadow. The whole keeping up appearances bullshit was starting to really wear on me.

Making my way down to the quiet basement was eerie; it felt like I had just walked in on everyone with their pants down.

"What's up?" I looked around the room, nervous as shit.

No one spoke. They were frozen, just staring at me.

Dane got up from his stool and turned me away from

everyone, wrapping one arm around my waist.

"Colt heard Mav call you Fallon," he whispered into my ear.

I gasped and froze.

Well damn it all to hell!

I put on the bravest smile I could, folded up my fake glasses, pulled off my suit jacket, and turned to the rest of the band and Serena.

"It's true." I sighed, defeated. That's the only way I could describe how I felt in that moment. The cat was out of its pesky bag and this crap could be really bad for me.

Rodney walked over and wrapped his arms around me tightly. "That's cool as shit, chick." He smiled and winked.

Colt rubbed a hand over the back of his neck, bouncing his jittering knee while he sat on his amp. "Fucking Fallon Dunbar in my fucking house and I didn't fucking know. What the..." He smiled at me.

Dane cleared his throat. "Well, this practice has been shot to shit. Anyone else hungry?"

"Fucking starving," Serena said, shoving off the couch and grabbing her purse. "There's this awesome burger joint across the street from the tattoo shop I work at."

All of us laughed in unison while she looked at us confused as hell. "What's so funny about burgers?"

Maverick smiled sweetly at her. "That's my dad's bar."

We all started to grab our coats to head out to eat when Dane stood on the first step in front of everyone. "This all might not seem like a huge deal to any of you, but *no one* can figure out that Fallon is who she really is. Outside of this group she *is* Fae Dunham. Got it?"

Everyone muttered and nodded; a calm washed over me knowing that I had a few more understanding friends in my corner.

Serena grabbed my hand and smiled at me. "We all have a past. I know you don't know me very well, but I promise I won't say a damn thing."

I gripped her hand and addressed everyone in the group. "Thanks."

It was such a small word for how big this all was for me. They all just nodded and there it was. I was finally among friends. Real friends, not the fake shit that comes along with fame. That was one of the sickest feelings in the world.

CHAPTER FIFTEEN

DEFINE FAMILY

DANE

"Hey, Pop!" I called over the bar to Marty. His back was to me, staring at half-empty liquor bottles on the back row of the bar doing inventory, clipboard in hand. The rest of the guys, Fallon, and Serena all started to take seats around a long table a few feet behind me.

The dark circles around Marty's light eyes and two day old scruff told all too much about how many hours he had been putting in at the bar. "Dane! Guys! It's not open mic night, to what do I owe this visit?"

Maverick slid onto the barstool next to me. "Worked up quite the appetite practicing tonight. Thought we'd stop in and grab a bite."

Marty nodded at his son. "Couple of pitchers of Pabst and nachos?"

"Sounds great, Pop. Thanks."

We started to head to the table when he cleared his throat. "You boys better be coming to this barbeque. Your mother has missed having a full house lately."

Maverick and I nodded in unison. "Yeah of course. We'll be there."

There was no way I would ever be able to repay Maverick and his family for what they did for me after my mom got locked up. Going to a family picnic was a very small price to pay for the years they took me in and helped restore my faith in humanity.

Dinner was over before we knew it. Surprisingly, even Serena was awesome to be around. The night went perfectly until I had to drop Fallon off at her apartment.

"Are you sure you don't want to come back to my place?"

Fallon shook her head while gripping the door handle. "Dane, I really like you and I want nothing more than to crawl into your ridiculously comfortable bed, but I have a mountain of work to tackle tomorrow. I am going to head into the office early so it's better if I stay here alone and get my ass to bed."

I popped out my lower lip and tried my best to put on sad puppy dog eyes. "Are you sure?" I got within an inch of her beautiful lips.

"Yes." She slowly pressed her lips onto mine, letting them linger tenderly before popping the door open and jumping out of the car.

She leaned in. "I'll see you tomorrow at work, babe."

Babe. That word rolling off her perfect pierced lips was incredibly sexy. I wanted to catch it in my mouth and crush my lips into hers.

"Alright." I sighed and the door slammed shut.

While walking up the stairs to my apartment, my phone buzzed in my pocket a few times. I checked my texts to find some I wanted to read and others, not so much.

Fallon: Thanks for a great night. Sitting in on that practice was freaking liberating. I needed that.

Whitney: Why have you been blowing me off and not responding to my texts?

Whitney: Are you fucking our new bitch of a boss?

Fallon: Let me know you got home safe.

Even though Whitney's texts made me see red and I would have loved to let her have it for calling Fallon a bitch, there was no way I was going to bark up the Whitney-crazy-tree at the moment. She was not going to ruin the amazing high I had from such a great night. So, I just rattled off a text back to Fallon.

Me: Just got to my place. Night, Juliet.

Fallon: Night, Romeo. Sweet dreams :*

I figured that the last bit was a kissy face and for the first time, seeing something so mushy didn't make me want to hurl. I started to walk down the hall to my apartment and froze right when I saw someone sitting in my doorway. In the dim light was the silhouette of the shell of a woman I used to know and love. It took everything in me to not turn and bolt down the stairs behind me. I wanted to scream and kill, but all I could do was choke out one word from my drying throat while my fists clenched and my entire body buzzed with rage.

"Mom?"

She slowly grappled to her feet and stared at me while I forced myself to yell, "What the fuck are you doing here?"

FALLON

I stepped out of my steaming shower, draping my body in a warm, fluffy towel. Walking around my apartment alone with dripping wet hair and pouring myself a small glass of wine to wind down usually didn't come with this terrible sting of loneliness, but there it was, nipping at my heels. All I wanted was to be in Dane's bed, drinking tea and cuddling under his warm comforter while he picked at his acoustic guitar. The sweet image made me want him even more.

Without thinking about it, I pulled on jeans, threw on a T-shirt, shoved my feet into my favorite pair of Uggs, and called for a cab. Within a few minutes I was in the backseat of a taxi, wrapped up warmly in a hoodie, riding the few blocks to Dane's apartment. If it weren't dark out I would have walked, but I was pretty afraid of the dark and being kidnapped. I was little and in my mind that meant that I was easily kidnap-able.

I practically ran up the stairs to Dane's apartment, hoping he wouldn't be mad that I was surprising him.

I knocked on the door and he answered quickly, leaning on the doorjamb, holding the door halfway shut. "What's up?" His voice was rough and shaky as he looked at the floor.

"I was lonely. I realized that I don't really care about a good night's sleep." I ran my fingers over his arm and he breathed in sharply.

"This really isn't a good—" A woman's voice called from inside, "Dane, honey, who is it?"

I saw red. My blood boiled. I was going to kick her fucking teeth in. I was going to kick his teeth in. I put my hand on the door, ready to shove it open, but Dane held on for dear-fucking-life.

"I said this is not a good time, Fallon." He growled through gritted teeth, pleading with his eyes as I leaned into the door with my shoulder, trying to force it open.

"Who the fuck is in there?" He wasn't getting off that easily.

"It's just a friend, *Mom*." Dane growled, locking his eyes on mine as my mouth fell open.

"Oh, honey. Let her in," the meek voice called again.

"I'm—" Dane put his hand on my shoulder, cutting off my apology.

"Don't worry about it. I was just about to make some tea. Want some?"

I nodded and Dane's head fell into a sigh as he opened up the door. Dane's mom got up from the couch, rubbing her hands on her jeans before walking up to me to introduce herself.

"Hi, I'm Claire." I took her frail hand.

"It's nice to meet you. I'm Fa-Fallon?" My voice turned up and I looked to Dane, who nodded. He had already used my real name, might as well go with it. Her light brown eyes had dark rings around them and her silver hair floated in wisps around her face. With hollow cheekbones, Claire smiled and nodded, taking the steaming mug out of Dane's hand.

"So, Mom." Dane's voice was so rigid, matching his posture as he took a seat in the armchair, the farthest spot from where Claire was sitting, forcing me to sit next to her on the couch. "How long have you been out?"

Her grip tightened on her mug as she stared into it, barely speaking louder than a whisper. "Just about a week."

Dane's face was stern and unreadable. There was so much I didn't know about their relationship, but I knew enough to be very concerned about the situation that was unfolding before me. I wanted to get to know Dane's mom, but I was pretty sure that would upset Dane.

"Where are you staying?" Dane's disdain dripped from each word. He was trying to hold something back, probably anger.

"On the other side of town. With a friend."

Dane laughed. "Is that what you're calling your drug dealer nowadays? A fucking *friend*?"

After setting her mug slowly down onto the coffee table, Claire hugged her jacket tighter around her body while her hands shook.

"Why are you really here, mother? Please don't say it's because you missed me."

"But I –"

She was cut off by Dane's sharp tongue lashing her. "If you missed me, you would have written, tried to apologize, or maybe entered the drug program I begged you to do after the state offered it to you."

"Dane, I've changed. I'm a new woman."

Dane got up and sat on the coffee table right in front of his mom, getting his face within a half-inch of hers. "Prove it." He grabbed her hand and yanked up her sleeves, revealing fresh track marks in the crook of her elbow.

"Fresh out and you couldn't *wait* to get a fucking fix. Get the fuck out of my home." Dane forcefully pulled her up from the couch and walked her right to the door.

"But I have nowhere else to go. No more money."

He opened the door and pushed her out of it. "Well you should have thought about that before you got Leilani in that fucking car with you. And by the way, if you don't leave, I will call the cops. I knew you'd be getting out soon so I filed a *no contact* against you. You're in violation right now. Your lawyer has a copy. Have a nice fucking life, Claire."

He slammed the door, resting his back on it and sliding down to the floor. He gently sobbed onto his knees, hugging his legs to his chest. I had no idea what to do, so I got down on the floor and held him while he cried softly in my arms.

"I fucking hate her," he mumbled.

"I know."

A few hard knocks sounded through the door and made me jump. Dane's grip on my shirt tightened. "She'll always be a junkie, wont she?"

Knock.

Knock, knock.

Bang, bang, bang.

"I hope not," I whispered, scared that she would be relentless.

Knock.

Knock.

"Did I do the right thing? Kicking her out?"

"Maybe." Chills ran up my arms while I pictured Claire

standing on the other side of the door, just as broken as her son.

Dane buried his hand into the crook of my neck, breathing in sharply before whispering, "I'm glad you showed up."

"Me too."

There was one final tap on the door and then silence. Dane and I stayed locked in one another's arms for what felt like hours, but in reality was only a few more minutes.

"Come on, let's get you to bed."

Dane took my hand and I helped him to his feet. The sadness and defeat that blanketed his face made my heart break.

CHAPTER SIXTEEN

ENJOY THE LITTLE THINGS

DANE

There was no sense in trying to sleep that night. I just held Fallon in my arms, her head cradled in the groove of my shoulder while she snored softly. Rage boiled through my entire body. It had all come crashing back down around me like it was yesterday.

Silence draped over me while my hands shook. I didn't know if it was more from the fear, sadness, or anger, or maybe all of it rolled into one heaping mess bottled up deep down inside my gut. Sitting in the sentencing hearing had been the hardest part of the process so far, and I really was not prepared for it in any way, shape, or form. Watching my mother stand before the judge moments before he was going to take away her freedom was simultaneously liberating and stifling. Maverick and Marty sat on either side of me. Their support and concern was palpable while hot tears stung the back of my eyes and my throat went dry.

The older judge cleared his throat and glanced around the

courtroom before speaking slowly, taking care to articulate each word. "Mrs. Pearson, I hereby sentence you to fifteen years..."

Those words echoed in my head while they filled the courtroom and time stood still. My eyes locked on my mother's as she slowly turned to me, her face tear-stained and scared. I could see her knees and hands shaking while sobs overcame her frail body. Her skin was chalky and seemed loose on her. Withdrawals had not been kind while the trial took place. I refused to post bail or let anyone else do it for us. She needed to pay for what she'd done and she needed to feel all of the pain of it, not hide behind a cloud of drugs and alcohol.

Marty leaned in, his hand on my shoulder. "Dane?"

I turned to him, my mouth open, tears falling rapidly. "Yeah?"

"Let's get you out of here, son." Marty pulled on my arm sternly.

That was the last day I had seen my mom before she showed up at my apartment hours before. It was all still an open wound with a frail bandage on it and there was no fixing that. There was really no light at the end of my tunnel of loathing.

Fallon shifted and rolled over, cuddling with my pillow. She looked so peaceful even though she was drooling a little, mouth completely open, hair matting to the side of her face. It shouldn't have been as attractive as it was, but it was. I stared, taking it all in: the way her small frame was swallowed up by my faded Hysterics shirt, which she had claimed for her sleeping attire every time she slept over. The way she was gripping on the pillow so tightly. How her eyes fluttered and her lips twitched while she softly snored. The way her lip rings glistened. It was all so hot. Add in her septum piercing and put a fork in me, I was fucking done.

I shifted under her, pulling her back onto my chest and holding her as tightly as I could without waking her. It was so simple and calming. In that moment I was broken and raw but there was nothing scary or painful about it; she took those horrible feelings away. I wasn't alone in this anymore, and that was the most amazing feeling I could have ever imagined.

Slowly my eyes closed, my mind stilled, and sleep was able to come, short and fleeting, but dreamless and fulfilling.

FALLON

"Dane?" I shook him a little while his phone alarm blared on the nightstand. "Dane, it's time to wake up."

He shifted groggily, releasing my waist to roll over and silence the terribly obnoxious siren screaming at us to get the hell out of bed. "I just want to lay right here all day," he mumbled before kissing my hair and wrapping his arms around me from behind.

"Well then." I shoved up from the bed and grabbed my purse off the floor. "Why don't we?"

I started a text to Payton, explaining that Dane and I needed a personal day. I knew that it would raise a few red flags with my boss-slash-pseudo uncle, but in that moment, I didn't give a rat's ass.

Dane grabbed my phone before I could hit the send button, his bloodshot eyes filled with concern and exhaustion. "You said you had a lot to do at work."

I shrugged, pulling the blanket over my bare legs. "It's freaking Friday and we work our asses off. We can afford to play hooky for one day."

Dane's lips slowly turned up at the corners, releasing my phone. I sent the text to Payton, and within a minute I got a message back.

Payton: Have a good day off. I hope everything is ok.

Simple as that.

Dane stretched slowly, yawning. His smile never faded while the yawn contorted his face and mouth. I giggled and kissed his chest before laying my head right where it had rested for most of the night.

"This is nice," I mumbled, wrapping my arms around his waist.

"Yeah, it sure is." He breathed, relaxing back onto his cushioned headboard.

There was a heaviness in Dane's breathing that reflected in his eyes. There was something biting at the back of his mind and I needed to help lift the weight.

"Spill."

His eyebrow rose while curiosity oozed out of each word. "What do you mean? Spill what?"

"What's on your mind?"

A deep breath entered his lungs through gritted teeth. He slowly exhaled while tightening his grip around me. "The first time I saw my mom smoke meth was when I was three. She got so high that she even offered the pipe to me. That's my first memory—ever. It was also the day my dad took off." He sighed. I kissed his cheek and he continued, "My favorite ice cream is rocky road. I hated the name The Hysterics when Rodney first suggested it, and still kind of wish we had brainstormed a little more on names. I tried to kill myself on the one year anniversary of my sister's death."

Even though sadness blanketed Dane's face, he seemed

lighter. Maybe sharing was more healing than I had thought, so it was my turn. With a deep breath, I dove in, "Regicide Assisted was my idea, the original name of my old band was Glass Eyed Fish." I rolled my eyes and laughed. "Such a dumb name."

Dane kissed my cheek. "What else? I want to know more about you."

I swallowed hard. "My favorite ice cream is rocky road, too. I miss my old life, but this one is growing on me."

Dane's lips brushed mine. "What else?"

"I can barely look my mom in the eye because I hate her for marrying my dad's partner. She's never admitted it, but I think they were having an affair before my dad was shot in the drive-by on my tenth birthday. Sam never really liked me because of all the times I accused them of screwing around. That's what started the abuse, along with his drinking."

"I'll kill him." Dane's voice was low, growling from deep in his gut.

"No need. He's a harmless old coward now."

"Can I hate him?"

I nodded, pulling the covers back over us. We held each other in silence until we both dozed off for a few more hours.

CHAPTER SEVENTEEN

BECOMING A LOCAL

FALLON

Dane snored lightly while my eyes fluttered open to see that the clock on the nightstand was blaring half past noon in bright red numbers. Even though there was nowhere for us to be, sleeping away the morning felt wrong. It was a terrible thing for a musician to be a morning person, but I felt guilty for sleeping away half of the day. The memory of my mom's voice squawked in my ears: *"We're burning daylight, Fal. Get a damn move on."*

My mother meant well, she really did have a kind heart, but she was totally brainwashed by Sam's callousness and controlling behavior. It only took a year from the day my father's body was put in the ground for Sam to move into our home, and within three months of that they were on their freaking honeymoon. It was safe to say I would never truly get over the way that felt. I missed my father. His warm smile. The way the crow's feet attached to the corners of his eyes would droop down when he cried happy tears at sappy commercials, even though he tried to hide how sentimental he truly was. The way his posture would be just a tad straighter once he was in his uniform. How no matter how late he had to work, he would always sneak into my room at night to wake me up and tell me a bedtime story, even if it was a short one.

I smiled at Dane's calm, sleeping face. There was so much about him that reminded me of my dad. They had identical hardass exteriors, hidden soft sides, and big hearts that loved with all their might.

Dane shifted, coughing a little, startling himself awake. I busted out laughing while he caught his breath looking like a deer caught in headlights.

"You ok?" I questioned, still laughing a little.

Wide-eyed, he nodded. "Just a bad dream."

"Oh yeah?"

"You know those dreams where you feel like you're falling?"

"I hate those!" They were the freaking worst and I had them all the time.

Right then my stomach rumbled *very* loudly. I blushed, wrapping my arms around my hollow stomach.

"I guess we should tame that beast."

I nodded. "That'd be nice."

"I know the perfect place! We need to make you a true Chicagoan sometime or another."

"You mean like a local?"

Dane shot up from the bed, reaching a hand out to help me to my feet. "Have you heard of Al's?"

I shook my head.

"You're in for a fucking treat then, babe." He winked, tossed me a small Hysterics shirt from the back of his closet, and started to put his sneakers on. "That's an extra, you can have it."

I pulled the guy's size small shirt over my head and pulled on my jeans. "So what is Al's, anyway?"

"You'll see. This is going to be epic."

After pulling my bedhead into a loose bun, attempting to make my smudged makeup look somewhat less vampire like, and praying that I wouldn't start smelling from the lack of deodorant, I slung my bag over my shoulder and entered Dane's living room where he was waiting. "Ready?"

He popped up from the couch and took my hand. "Heck yes." A smile that could light up the entire city spread across Dane's stubble covered face. His eyes were bright with excitement and I breathed in their infectious brilliance. My skin tingled as our fingers interlaced and I rose up on my tiptoes to kiss his soft grinning lips. I wanted to catch his amazing energy and harness it, let it course through my callous veins and bring me back to life. Right in that moment, I wanted nothing more than to truly be alive in my new life.

As the clock rolled around to one, we were walking up to Al's. A gigantic sign screamed brilliantly on an awning over a small modest restaurant: 'Al's #1 Italian Beef'.

The grip on my hand tightened while Dane's excited gaze dropped down to mine. "This is the original."

"There's more of Al around?" I was trying to be funny

through my naiveté and Dane just kissed the top of my head and nodded.

For being famous and having the number one Italian beef sandwich, the inside was just as modest as the outside, and frankly, kind of underwhelming. We were greeted by a young guy behind a wood paneled counter with a face filled with acne, probably the result of eating too many greasy sandwiches.

Dane smiled at the pimply-faced kid and rattled off, "We'll take two beefs, dipped with hot and sweet."

"Any fries or drinks?"

"Two pops and an order of fries."

The guy rang us up and gave us our soggy, messy-looking sandwiches faster than I could have said lickety-split.

"Alright, I have to teach you how to eat this." Dane was still grinning ear to ear while I looked at him like he had six heads.

"Ok? I mean, I have eaten a sandwich one or two times in my lifetime."

He rolled his eyes. "Not like a true Chicagoan. Come here."

We walked over to the counter with our backs facing the counter where we had ordered. Dane set our food out and took the drinks from me, setting them down and grabbing my hips.

"You have to plant your feet here." He shifted me to the perfect spot, which felt way too far away from the counter.

"Ok," he continued, standing right next to me, "Now put your forearms like this on the bar." He leaned his forearms onto the edge of the counter and waited for me to follow suit.

"And then lean over so that if you spill, nothing gets on you, just on the counter or floor."

"The floor? I'm not a heathen!"

Dane chuckled, sliding my beef sandwich—which was dripping with a crazy amount of juice—in front of me. "Trust me, this is how everyone does it!"

I shrugged. "Alright. Here goes nothing." I grabbed my overstuffed, soggy bun and dove in. *Holy hell.* It was the most amazingly spicy, sweet, soggy, delicious explosion of flavor I could have ever hoped to sink my teeth into.

"Well?" Dane was waiting for my reaction, not even touching his meal.

My eyes grew wide and my smile started to curl. "This is fucking incredible!"

Dane nodded. "See, I told you!"

DANE

After using a ton of napkins and almost covering my shirt in gravy, the last bite of phenomenal beef was rolling around in my mouth.

"You ready?" Fallon's cute lips sucked on her straw and I felt my dick twitch.

Fuck, she's too damn hot. Is there such a thing?

My mind focused on ripping the T-shirt off of her and fucking her gorgeous body right on the bar at Al's.

She nudged my arm with an elbow and I choked out, "Yeah.

Let's blow this pop stand."

She laughed at my dumb cliché and grabbed her bag.

"You should probably take me home."

Ugh. Terrible words to hear, but she was right. "Alright." I pouted, opening The Judge's door for her to slide into the passenger seat.

"Why so serious, Romeo?"

"It's the worst part of my day—leaving you."

She popped out her bottom lip, trying to feign a frown. "Doesn't absence make the heart grow founder?"

I shrugged my shoulders. "That's not a risk I'm willing to take."

Man, I'm fucking sappy. Chicks like sappy, right? Fallon seemed to be enjoying it at least.

"Well, I do have practice tonight."

"See, I'd just cramp your rock star style!" she giggled. Her giggle was adorable, way too freaking cute for me to not hear all the fucking time, like every minute of every damn day.

"I think the guys would love to enjoy your presence again."

She rolled her eyes, buckling her seatbelt and taking the door handle into her hand. "Get in," she demanded and I trotted around the front end of my amazingly gorgeous car.

I let the engine rumble to life, taking Fallon's small hand in mine. "I will take you home and not be too needy." I knew I was taking up too much of her time, that I was being too pushy, but I was falling fast and she was my only safety net.

She leaned over to kiss my cheek. "I'll be going to the barbecue tomorrow. One night won't kill us, babe. Promise."

"Well if you promise, who am I to question you?"

I was the last one to show up to practice.

"Hey, guys." I slumped onto the stool behind my set.

"Hey, Dane. You all right?"

There was nothing wrong with me. I was fucking fantastic. But the little kid from "Love Actually" came to mind, specifically when he was sitting on the park bench with his stepfather and saying, "Worse than the total agony of being in love?" That little kid was right: love was total agony. Fantastic agony.

"Yeah, of course I am."

"Why didn't you bring Fallon? She could really help us."

"She wanted to have a night to catch up on some work. Can we just get this shit started?" I sounded pissed and bratty, which was not my intention at all; I was just preoccupied.

We dove into one of the first songs that Maverick had ever written. I loved the lyrics, the angst and lust behind them. It was captivating and fast-paced and raw. There wasn't any truth to the words that wove together to tell a sad story of toxic lovers, but it was so convincing. Maverick was just that talented.

There's a pain clicking inside my heart

Keeping it locked away behind my lips

Influenced by a secret hidden deep down from you

You think you know me

I want to believe all the lies you know and trust

The words bleed from my mouth

And they are the poison

Eating at my heart

As it kills you slowly in my arms

I'm your killer

I'm your lover

This is a corrupt utopia

You call perfect

And I call hell

I love your smile

And how you're always carefree

I hate what I do to you

Take your world, twist it into sugar and spoon feed you bliss

When the reality is salt stinging the cuts caused by my claws

Pure white turned to battlefields of red

Running dry from our two day old duel

The flames getting blown out from your eyes

A birthday cake wish dying as you give in

After reluctantly dropping Fallon off, barely being able to

concentrate at practice, taking a long shower, and chowing down on some amazing Chinese delivery, I was fucking bored out of my skull. Fallon was running around in my brain, so I shot off a text to her.

Me: Twenty questions? You start...

Fallon: Game on! What's your favorite time of year?

Me: Fall. What's your favorite thing to sleep in?

Fallon: The Hysterics shirt I stole from you. If you could write a letter to your seventeen-year-old self but it could only be two words, what would it say?

Me: Keep believing. What is the one thing you wish you could take back?

Fallon: The last time I did coke. What is your favorite recent memory?

Me: The day you walked into our office for the first time. What do you wish you could change about yourself?

Fallon: My lack of confidence. What is your favorite feeling?

Me: Too vague...

Fallon: Come on...it can be anything.

Me: Alright, the moment I have a fresh pair of sticks in my hands, the electricity of euphoria. What is one thing you miss?

Fallon: That exact feeling.

That's all she wrote. There it was: I'd crossed the line, hit a nerve, pushed her to an edge. I had no idea what Fallon was going through or why she was in this self-imposed limbo of hiding.

Me: Why are you Fae Dunham?

Fallon: Because that was the only way I could truly live again. Sleep well, Dane.

Me: Alright, you too.

She was running again and I couldn't blame her. There were so many layers left of her onion that I needed to peel. Yeah, Shrek was on my TV and Donkey had just referred to parfaits having layers too, so it seemed fitting. Either way, whether Fallon was a parfait or an onion, it was all mysterious and confusing and addicting.

CHAPTER EIGHTEEN

WALLS OF STEELE

DANE

"Hey, man," I answered my phone as I drove to the Steele's home.

Maverick's voice came through the receiver. "Hey, you're on your way, right?"

"Yeah, why? What's up?"

"Nah, nothing. Just making sure. I got here about ten minutes ago and we're pretty much set. Can you pick up a couple bags of ice and a case of beer? I'm worried we'll run out."

"Sure. Any particular beer?"

"Nah. You know we're not picky."

"Ok. Pabst it is."

"Ha, should've guessed."

"It's tradition."

"True. See you soon."

"Later."

I stopped into the gas station just down the road from the home I'd lived in for the last two years of high school and the first year of college. I sent a quick text to Fallon.

> **Me: I'm about to be at the Steele's to help set up. I'll be by in an hour or so to pick you up.**

> **Fallon: You don't have to come all the way back here to get me. I'll take a cab.**

> **Me: No, it's not a big deal. I'll text you when I'm on my way.**

> **Fallon: What's the address?**

> **Me: Man, you're stubborn, huh?**

> **Fallon: As a fucking mule. What's the address?**

I gave in and hit the send button as nerves rushed in. Fallon was about to meet the rest of my family, or at least what I considered family. All I could do was hope that they all made a good impression on her, and vice-versa. The Steeles all had a way of opening their big mouths that never painted things in the best light. The cashier rang me up for the case of beer, twenty bucks worth of gas, and the bags of ice.

By the time I was pulling into the already crowded driveway I could barely keep my knee from bouncing and my heart from racing. Before I was even out of the car Maverick was opening the privacy fence's gate so I didn't have to go all the way through the house.

"Thanks." I handed one of the bags to Maverick.

"Sure. Where's Fallon—I mean Fae. Shit, what do we call her

here?"

"For today she's Fae. She's finishing up some edits and then she'll be on her way."

Maverick nodded. "Gotcha."

"All the time she is Fae, unless we tell you otherwise." My voice was sterner than I meant it to be, but Fallon cared a lot about her façade and I wasn't going to be the one that screwed it all up for her.

"Alright, man. Don't get your panties in a bunch."

I stopped halfway up the front lawn. "Dude, this shit is really freaking important. It's her life, everything she has worked so hard to build from the ashes, and she needs our support."

Maverick put his free hand on my shoulder. "You really like her, don't you?"

I stared at the ground and nodded.

Maverick sighed. "It's more than that, isn't it?"

I nodded again.

"I'm happy for you."

"Thanks," I muttered, walking through the open gate to be greeted by Chester, the Steeles' newest family member. After Maverick and I moved out and Julie moved back in with her five-year-old daughter, Alex, Maverick's mom decided that they needed a puppy. She went out with Alex and let her pick out anything in the pet store she wanted, and of course the five-year-old picked a freaking Saint Bernard—yep, a Beethoven. A huge, furry, loving goofball. At only eight months, Chester was a whopping ninety-seven pounds and as clumsy as he could be. He lunged at me, tail wagging a mile a minute, practically knocking me off my feet while happily whimpering.

"Chester, bad doggy!" Alex's sweet voice tried to lower like the dog trainer had told her so she could 'assert her dominance'. What a load of crap—Chester was three times the size of Alex. Then a shrill cry came from the small child, "Uncle Dane!"

I dropped the ice and case of beer at my sides and knelt down so my small goddaughter could jump into my arms for a big bear hug. "Hi, sweetheart!" I pressed her to my chest, breathing in the sweet smell of coconut shampoo. "I missed you."

"I missed you, too! Why don't you come to play anymore?" There wasn't a good enough answer to satisfy a five-year-old when it came to real-life-grown-up-stuff, it just didn't make sense.

"I'm sorry. I'll try to do better."

"You better." A familiar singsong voice came from behind me and I spun around with Alex still in my arms to see her mom, Julie, smiling at me. "Hi, Dane."

Man, was Julie a sight for sore eyes. After Leilani died, we were all wrecks, but Julie understood it the best out of everyone; Leilani and her had been attached at the hip ever since they could walk.

"It's so good to see you." I set Alex down and was shocked to see how much more she was looking like her mom as she got older: they had the same dusting of freckles just over their noses and cheeks, big bright hazel eyes, and strawberry blonde hair.

Julie and I hugged for longer than most people would feel comfortable, but that was us. For a while I thought that I loved Julie as more than just a friend, but she never returned the affection and ran off to Wisconsin with some Army guy right after high school. She wound up catching the dirt bag cheating on her with strippers, in their bed, right after finding out she was pregnant with Alex.

We all made our way to the large wood deck where a long

table with finger foods and small sandwiches were lined up along with three coolers full of beer and pop at the end. Maverick's mom was busily straightening out the table while Marty tied his famous 'Kiss the Cook' apron around his waist.

"I guess it's grilling time already?"

Marty and Gina promptly turned to me, huge grins proudly resting on their faces. Gina grabbed each side of my face, pulling me closer to her. I stumbled a few steps while she planted a forceful, red lipstick filled kiss on my forehead. "It's been too long," she scolded, releasing my face. "Where's the girl? Maverick said you were bringing someone."

I pulled my lips together. "Yeah, she'll be here soon." This was the first time I had ever brought a girl around my pseudo parents—ever.

"This is big!" Her eyes were wide while she patted my shoulder. "It's great!"

Marty and I did the guy half hug thing as he asked, "Medium rare like always?"

"You got it, Pop."

I cracked open a beer and took a seat in one of the metal chairs around the large round glass table next to the grill where Maverick was already sitting with his feet up on another chair. He wore his old wrestling shirt from high school with a faded pair of jeans, and was gently picking an acoustic guitar and singing to Alex, who was sitting on the floor petting Chester.

Julie sat down on the other side of me. "What time are the rest of the guys coming?" Her voice was jittery, not a sound I was familiar with from her.

I shrugged. "You know them, they operate in a different time zone than normal society."

She nodded. "Sheils will be here soon. And so will Aunt Greta and her latest *friend*." Julie raised an eyebrow and lowered her voice. "She *finally* came out!"

"No way!"

I had known since the first Christmas I spent with the Steeles that Gina's little sister by fifteen years batted for the other team, but no one ever talked about that taboo subject and everyone was scared of upsetting Gina.

"I know! I just can't believe Mom's ok with her bringing her you-know-what to this shindig!"

"So, get this." I swallowed the lump forming in my throat; I needed to get this out sooner than later. "Claire showed up on my doorstep last night."

Everyone froze. Maverick set the guitar down, Julie's hand flew to my arm and gripped tightly, Gina shrieked, and Marty dropped his grilling tongs. They all just stared, wide-eyed, waiting for me to continue. Thankfully, I was saved by the bell—well, the doorbell anyway.

"I'll get it. And don't worry, she won't be bothering any of us."

"Dane—what?" Gina's hands were on her hips and her face was riddled with concern.

"I filed a *no contact*, she can't come near me."

Everyone sighed in unison.

"Do you all really think I would do something to hurt her?"

"Didn't you?" Maverick shrugged as I jokingly flipped him the bird while Alex was jumping onto her mom's lap.

I popped up from my chair, retreating into the house to answer the door for the one person I wanted there more than anything else.

"I'm so glad to see you." I scooped Fallon into my arms in the doorway, her arms slowly folding around my waist.

"Is everything ok?" she breathed into my ear.

I nodded, our cheeks pressed together. "It is now."

FALLON

It is now—my thoughts exactly.

Those words swam around in my head as I stood in the doorway wrapped in Dane's arms. Being without him for only twelve or so hours had felt like a lifetime. I had never been so dependent on someone else for happiness and clarity and it scared the shit out of me.

I breathed in the faint hint of Dane's cologne. "Aren't you going to invite me in?"

"Oh, right." Dane's face perked up. He took my hand and led me out back to the deck where the smell of burgers sizzling and the music of lighthearted laughter were absolutely uplifting.

First Dane walked me over to a woman who looked to be in her mid-fifties. She had a long bob haircut with the slightest hint of gray in her light blonde hair, bright blue eyes, and the widest smile I had ever seen. We stood at the same eye level as Dane introduced us. "Fae, this is Gina, Maverick's mother."

She reached her arms out, and without hesitating, I was hugging Mrs. Steele. "Dane has told me so much about you, Gina."

"It is so nice to meet you, dear."

A sweet voice chimed in, "Hi, Fae? I'm Julie, Mav's sister."

We hugged and I was introduced to Alex, the most adorable little girl I had ever met in my life. She was towing a huge puppy by its leash—or maybe it was the other way around. After saying hi to Maverick and Marty, it hit me: the little girl in the photo at Dane's apartment was Alex.

With that a rush of people came through the sliding glass door. Colt brought Serena, who was her usual bouncy bubblegum self, and his sister, Sheila, who was apparently Julie's best friend. Rodney showed up with a date on his arm. It took me a couple minutes to place where I had seen her before, but once she said hi to me I realized she was the chick from the open mic night, Candice.

"Here comes trouble," Dane snickered in my ear while I watched a short, plump, butch woman walk out the door hand in hand with a tall must-be-a-model woman. She had the most gorgeous mocha skin I had ever seen. Awkward pleasantries were exchanged between Maverick's whole family and the two newcomers. Dane whispered the gossip in my ear about the shorter one being Greta, Gina's little sister, and that Greta had finally come out a little over a year ago. He said she had been living with her girlfriend—who actually was a model—for a few years in secret. He explained that everyone knew that Greta was gay, that it was really the lying and secrecy that bothered Gina so much.

With the party in full swing and my mind buzzing with all of the new faces and names, I found myself sitting on a bench on the far side of the deck with Sheila and Julie. They were both amazingly sweet and continued to try to guide the conversation so I could comfortably join in.

"Do you remember that time when Leilani accidentally

ratted Dane out for skipping class to go to that underground music festival?"

Julie and Sheila both started laughing uncontrollably. It was sweet, watching them reminisce about Dane's childhood, a small glimpse into a side of him that he kept buried deep under sadness and hate.

"So, Fae, how is it being Dane's boss?" Julie sipped on her lemonade through a straw while smiling with her eyes.

I shrugged. "Pretty great. Dane's incredibly talented and Raging Underground is an awesome place to work."

Sheila nodded. "Being a journalist must be so exciting."

"It can be. I haven't been doing it for too long."

Shit. I'm saying too much.

"What were you doing before?" It was an innocent enough question for Julie to ask, keeping the conversation flowing and all, but it sent my heart racing and my palms started to itch.

"Food's ready," Marty called over our way. "Girls, come get it before it gets cold."

After we all chowed down on some amazing burgers and Alex showed me her Barbie Dream House. I wound up sitting on the couch with Gina, sipping coffee while Dane and Maverick insisted on doing all of the dishes. Sheila and Julie were reading Alex a bedtime story and the rest of the gang was sitting around a crackling fire in the backyard.

"Dane's something else, isn't he?" Gina smiled at me while she straightened up a stack of magazines on the coffee table in front of us.

"He sure is."

"We're lucky to have him. After his mom went away, I was

worried the state was going to take him from us. It was a fight but we all got through it, only slightly battered and bruised." Her warm eyes showed so much love and pride.

"I can't imagine it was easy, opening up your home to another teenaged boy."

"It was a challenge, but Dane was always part of the family, even before everything that happened. Leilani too."

"I kind of got that feeling from how fondly your daughter and Sheila speak about Leilani. It's really touching."

"Promise me something?" She looked right into my eyes, her hand on my knee.

"Sure?"

"If you can't love him completely, then don't love him at all."

"I'm sorry?"

"If you can't love the baggage and scars and messed up bullshit along with his kind heart, then don't drag his heart through the mud."

Her words sank in.

Festered.

Burned.

We just sat there in silence staring at each other for a few seconds until Dane walked up with both of our coats in hand. "Ready to head out?"

I blinked a few times before looking up at him. "Ye-Yeah. It was very nice to meet you, Gina. Thank you for having me." My words sounded rehearsed, almost robotic, but it was the best I could do.

"It was a pleasure, dear." She hugged me lightly.

Dane led the way into the backyard where we said our

goodbyes to the group then headed to his apartment.

My world was flipped around and I couldn't ground myself. Gina was right; I was scared of commitment and it wasn't fair to drag Dane into my fucked up life. It was better to not get too attached—it would only hurt more later.

"Dane, we need to talk."

"Ok." He slouched onto his couch, patting the seat next to him.

I took it, but didn't lean into his shoulder like usual.

"Is everything ok?"

I shook my head.

"Fuck."

His knee started bouncing.

My voice shook. "I just don't know what to make of all this."

"What do you mean?"

"This." I motioned back and forth between us. "It's all happening so fast, and I don't do *this*. Like, ever. This isn't me."

"Well, who are you then?"

His words were rough; I didn't know anymore.

I shrugged.

"Fallon." He sighed, rubbed the back of his neck, then continued, "I don't know what's happening either. But I know I want it. Do you?"

I nodded, but I wasn't sure.

"Ok, look. Here's how I see it." He shifted off the couch and got on his knees in front of me, making me look into his steel gray eyes while he laced his fingers with mine. "You're a damaged, erratic, closed-off mess and I love every bit of you for it."

"You love me?"

It was strange to hear that someone loved me and know they really meant it. I hadn't felt that since my dad died.

He nodded.

"I love you, too." The words barely made a sound as they leapt from my throat, like a fleeting wind. I was scared to more than whisper them, afraid they might run away.

We sat wrapped in silence. There are times when more is understood in silence than words can ever say. I wasn't going anywhere and neither was he. Baggage—fucked up commitment issues, weird identity crises, deep family tragedy—all of it. We were supposed to be together. We were soulmates. Until that moment I had thought that a soulmate was a mythical creature, not something that happened in real life. I was wrong; mine was staring right at me, into me, loving me for who I was deep down.

CHAPTER NINETEEN

EAVESDROPPING

DANE

Monday morning came way too soon, especially since another meeting was just finishing and the clock barely read nine. Our latest publication had increased our subscribers by over thirty percent. Payton was, of course, beyond thrilled, and this morning meeting was how he decided to reward us. Once it was over, Fallon waved me over. Her eyes sparkled through her fake glasses.

"What's up?" I questioned, getting close enough to smell her perfume. *Fuck.* She smelled good enough to lick, right on the spot, in the middle of this damn boardroom full of nosy journalists.

"I need to see you in my office." She bit one of her lip rings, trailing her fingertips slowly over my tie. "Now," she growled.

I nodded. "S-sure." I swallowed while willing my half chub to cool his jets before I could get safely behind the closed door of Fallon's office.

Payton stopped Fallon right as we were about to walk through the door. "Fae? Have a second?"

She nodded. I damned her under my breath for it, but what else was she supposed to do?

"Dane, I'll be right in. Pull up that article you wanted me to look at."

I took the hint from the slight wink she gave me and hurried into her office. Sliding into one of the plush red chairs in front of Fallon's desk, I sighed and waited. It didn't take more than a few minutes for Fallon to return and shut her office door, concealing us from the rest of our coworkers.

"Is everything ok?"

Fallon nodded as she slowly walked over to me, taking off her jacket and throwing it onto her chair across the desk. "He knows about us."

The flatness in her voice was troubling. "Isn't that a bad thing?"

She shook her head. "Payton is on my side."

"Ok...?"

"We have to make this quick. I have a meeting in a few minutes."

Fallon crawled into my lap and straddled me, slowly planting small kisses on my neck right below my ear. The worry of the boss knowing or caring about our relationship completely dissipated as I started to unbutton Fallon's light pink blouse. Hastily, she unclasped my belt and yanked my boxers and pants down. My erection sprang to attention as she hiked her skirt up.

"Wait." I stopped her as she started to pull up her skirt.

"What?"

173

"Do you have a condom?"

"I'm on birth control. You are clean, aren't you?"

I had never been with someone without a condom, ever, but I got checked regularly, so I nodded. Fallon hastily pushed her tiny thong to the side and took in my length. Every nerve in my body buzzed. The sheer pleasure of truly feeling her was incredible.

A low growl escaped the back of my throat as I clasped one hand tightly over Fallon's mouth and the other reached under the thin lace of her bra to cup her supple breast. She lightly bit down on my palm as she rode my dick faster and faster while the corners of her eyes watered. Her climax built up in the back of her eyes as our lips locked. Her hand ran through my hair, gripping tightly as her pussy tightened around my shaft. I felt her release; her low groans and whimpers quickly sent me over the edge as I thrust into her as hard as I could. My dick throbbed as I released inside of her, my entire body shuddering while a thin layer of sweat formed on my brow.

Fallon started to pant as I released her mouth and her head fell to my chest. I leaned back into the plush chair, eyes fixating on the dark blue quill etched beautifully around Fallon's collarbone and shoulder.

"You're so fucking perfect," I breathed, taking in how amazingly sexy Fallon was: straddling me with her blouse open, exposing her gorgeous boobs propped up in her black lace bra, her hard nipples poking through the thin fabric.

A light tap came from the door.

Fuck.

We both jumped up.

Fallon hurriedly buttoned her blouse while I finished straightening my tie and fixed my belt.

The doorknob turned a little too early—to say the least. The wide eyes of the last person I wanted to see stared right at me.

"Whitney," Fallon choked. "You're a little...early." Fallon stared at me while I smoothed out the wrinkles in my shirt.

"Early bird gets the worm, right?" There was no mistaking the hiss in her voice.

"Dane, will you excuse us?" Fallon sat behind her desk with pleading eyes.

I wanted to say 'fuck no'. Instead, I just mumbled, "Sure."

"I think he'd like to stay for this." Whitney patted the chair next to hers. I walked around Fallon's desk and stood behind her, my hand resting on her tensed shoulder.

"What is it?" Fallon's voice was strained and low as we both stared at the pages clutched in Whitney's hand.

"Here." Whitney's face twisted into a deviously maniacal smile as her eyes narrowed. A satisfied smirk spread across her face as she watched our mouths fall open.

The headline read 'The Ghost Among Us: Fallon Dunbar'.

Nervously, I busted out laughing. Fallon's gaze shot up to me, terror running across her face as tears started to well. Whitney shot me a death stare.

"Do you really think you can threaten me like this?" Fallon snarled.

"Yes." Whitney folded her arms over her chest, cocking her head to the side. "I will personally hand this to Payton and destroy you, sweetie."

Now it was Fallon's turn to laugh. "Let's tell Payton ourselves." Fallon's voice cooed into the speaker on her desk, "Missy, ask Payton to come to my office, please?"

Payton's sweet assistant chirped into the line, "Right away, Ms. Dunham."

Within a few minutes Payton was striding into the small office, wide-eyed as he glanced at each person in the room.

"Fae? You needed me?"

"Yes, sir. Whitney has an interesting little tidbit to share."

Payton took the seat next to Whitney, angling himself to be able to look directly at her. "Is that so, Ms. Quints?"

Whitney cleared her throat, her hands shaking. "Ya-Yes, sir."

"Well, out with it. I don't have all day."

"You see, the other night I went to Dane's apartment to ask him to look over an article I wrote." She paused and my mind screamed *Bullshit!*

"A woman ran out of his apartment crying before I could get to the door and said that he was with a young woman by the name of Fallon. It all clicked, sir." Her gaze was locked on the dark burgundy carpet as we all stared at her, our eyes boring holes in her.

Fallon chimed in, "Yes, that woman would be Dane's mother, who he had just had a fight with."

Payton chuckled a few times. "Ms. Quints, I want to advise you to not poke your nose in others' affairs."

"Sir?" Whitney was shocked as Payton pointed to her article on the desk.

"You see, everyone in this business has a past. What kind of boss would I be if I allowed rumors to fly from the mouth of a druggie all the way to ruining a valued member of my staff's reputation? Has Fae been anything but kind to you?"

Whitney shook her head.

"Has Fae demonstrated anything other than a professional attitude while behind these walls?"

She shook her head again.

"Explain." Payton was starting to lose his patience with her and she knew it.

"They were in here fooling around before my meeting."

"Do you have proof?"

She just sat there.

"Would it really matter if Fae were to end up being Fallon Dunbar?"

She shook her head.

"Very good then. You may leave, unless Fae has anything else to add?"

Fallon nodded. "Please leave this article. I think it could very well be the best piece you've written."

Whitney smiled sheepishly and hurriedly scurried out the door, tail between her legs.

Once the door was shut, Payton cleared his throat. "Fallon? Are you ok?"

She nodded, wiping a tear from her cheek. "That was a close one."

"Are you still sure this is the right choice?"

She nodded slowly. I was still a freaking statue, trying to make sense of all of the bull that had just flown through the office.

"Alright then. Next time the two of you need some alone time, do it when people aren't snooping around like alley cats."

"Sorry."

Payton winked and for the first time since he'd walked into the office, his gaze shifted to mine. "You better take care of her."

I exhaled, finally relaxing. "I will."

Paton left us and I fell into the chair he had just vacated. "Payton knew all along?"

Fallon's face said it all.

"Why didn't you tell me?"

"It didn't seem important."

"I've been walking on eggshells trying to watch myself around here and you didn't think I'd like to know that the only other person that knew about your secret was someone I talked to every day, let alone my boss?"

"Can we just drop this for now?"

I sighed. "Yeah, sure. Do you want to come over tonight before my practice?"

"That sounds really nice."

Finally, a smile started forming at the corners of Fallon's pierced lips.

"Good." I got up, made my way over to Fallon, and grabbed her shoulders. "I love you." It was a statement that I needed to voice more often even though I didn't always have the courage.

"I love you, too." Relief settled into Fallon's eyes and I went back to work with very little productivity, way too preoccupied by what I was going to do during lunch.

I typed up a text to Maverick.

Me: Are we still on for one?

Maverick: Sure thing, brother.

Me: Perfect, I only have an hour for lunch.

Maverick: No worries, my guy knows we're coming. It'll be quick.

Me: Awesome

Maverick: You sure you're ready?

Me: I've never been more sure of anything in my entire life.

Maverick: Good enough for me.

FALLON

We didn't make it more than two steps into Dane's apartment before we got into the conversation I had been dreading since the episode in my office earlier that day.

Dane and I sat on the couch and he grabbed my shoulders, concern and curiosity swimming in his gaze. "What does it matter, Fallon? Who will it really hurt if you come out and say who you really are?"

"You just don't fucking get it, do you? Any of it!" I barked. I didn't want to talk about it anymore. It was over. I was Fae. It was the bed I'd made and I needed to lie in it.

He shook his head, defeated, letting his hands fall from my shoulders. "No," he muttered, diverting his gaze to my trembling hands.

"It's me. It will hurt me."

He stared at me, mouth open, silent.

I took a few short breaths, cleared my throat, and decided to be honest for the first time since this whole Fae Dunham shitstorm had started. I wanted to be honest—not just with Dane, but with myself as well. "I'm scared of the person I became. Fallon is dead and I need her to be. What she was, what she did, what she was capable of—it all died that night in the bathroom of that cheap ass motel. When I woke up in that hospital bed, Sam yelling at me for being a selfish prick and my mom crying so hard it looked like she was convulsing, I knew I needed to make huge changes. I hated Fallon, but I couldn't live with hating myself anymore. I thought that being Fae would fix it."

I paused and grabbed Dane's hands in mine. "It didn't fix it," I whispered.

"Then what do we do?"

"Don't you see?"

He shook his head.

"I'm too far down this rabbit hole to climb out. There's no saving Fallon and Fae. I have to choose one and be done with the other."

Dane wrapped me in his arms as his husky voice softly whispered, "I don't care what your name is, who you pretend to be, or if you come clean. None of that matters. I am in love with who you are behind closed doors, when we're alone. Deep down, you are the girl of my dreams. I love you. Marry me."

With that, he pulled a small box out of his pocket, shifted off the couch, and knelt in front of me. "You don't have to pretend anymore. You won't have to hide behind a name that you don't want or one you made up. Take mine. Take me."

All I could do was nod with tears streaming and mouth a yes

as he slipped the beautiful white gold band with a haloed square stone onto my left ring finger.

"I love you." My shaky voice cracked and I gripped Dane's shirt, pulling his lips to mine. "Of course I'll marry you! Yes!"

"I love you, too."

I glanced over at the clock on the wall. "Dane, you have to get to practice." He was already supposed to be at Colt's house.

"Come with me." He got up from the floor, extending his hand to me.

"Ok." I got up, staring at the sparkling diamonds glimmering brilliantly on my hand. It didn't feel real. I didn't feel like I deserved any of this, but here it was, here he was, and holy crap—it was perfect.

We rushed down Colt's basement steps to find the rest of the band members sitting on the old couch, waiting for us and slowly clapping as we made our way into the dim room. I heard a bottle of champagne pop as they rushed over to hug both Dane and me, and everyone yelled, "Congratulations!"

"Thanks, guys."

"Welcome to the family, Fallon." Maverick kissed me on the cheek before wrapping me in a huge bear hug.

"Thanks."

"Alright, alright, let's get to work." Dane was beaming, standing next to his drum set. He winked at me while I took a seat on the lumpy couch.

I snapped a picture of my ring, captioned it 'HOLY SHIT!' in a text to Starr, and waited patiently for her to respond.

I swayed to the melody of a beautiful ballad, Dane's eyes never leaving mine as he mouthed the words.

Stop my heart, inspire me

Take my breath away

Make me believe

I know there is beauty, I want to see yours

Be raw, open up

Let me see everything

Walk along the thin line of sanity

Dark and deep, cool and damp

The caverns of your soul

Ones left unexplored

That's where I belong

Cloak me in your imagination

Let me take it all in

Stop my heart, inspire me

Take my breath away

Make me believe that you love me

My phone buzzed in my hand, showing Starr was calling. "Excuse me, it's Starr."

They all nodded. I ran up the stairs and out to the front porch to sit in a wooden rocker. "Hey!"

"Holy fuck balls! What just happened?" Starr was screaming at an octave that only dogs could hear clearly.

"I found a guy."

"No shit, Sherlock!"

"Pretty crazy, huh?"

"I'd say so!"

"I wish you were here."

"Me, too. I'll plan a trip up soon! I have to meet this..." She trailed off, waiting for me to finish with Dane's name. I couldn't believe it had been that long since Starr and I had talked, and it really made me feel crappy.

"Dane. His name is Dane. He is the drummer in a local band. I'm actually at their practice now."

"Does he know?"

"Yes, he knows who I am."

"Good. Then, as of right now, until further judgment is made, I approve!"

I giggled. "That's a relief."

"I gotta run, we're trying out a new drummer tonight."

My heart ached. "Yeah, ok. Good luck."

"They'll never be you."

"I know. I'm sorry."

"Don't be. You're happy, that's what really matters."

"I love you."

"Love you, too, bitch."

DANE

Fallon made her way back down into the basement right as Colt took a call from our booking agent. I motioned for her to come and sit on my lap. She did, and right as her weight shifted onto me and her lips planted a gentle kiss on my cheek, my heart started pounding and I was up on fucking cloud nine. That ring on her finger, her right there, it was all just so right.

"Ok, that is incredible! Thank you for letting me know. Uh huh. Yes, of course we'll be there." Colt was pacing around the couch, biting his nails like he always did when he was nervous. When the call ended, Colt stopped in his tracks and just stared at his phone.

"Colt?" Maverick threw an empty water bottle, hitting Colt in the shoulder. His eyes shot up, wide as a slow smile rolled onto his lips. "Gonna tell us what Danny said?"

He looked down at his hands, which he clenched and unclenched nervously, his face as red as a college girl who'd just returned from Keith Richard's hotel room. After a moment, he looked up at us again, still unsure of what to say. "Um." The pacing started again, Colt's eyes darting from the blackened screen on his phone over to us.

"Come on, man, you're acting like a teenaged girl who just saw One Direction walk across the street." Rodney started laughing at Maverick's comment and Colt finally snapped out of it.

"Well, you see, I heard a few days ago that a few of the bands had to pull out of the Underground Music Fest coming up this weekend." Colt took a few slow, deep breaths. "And Danny just called to let me know that we got one of the slots."

"What?" I jumped to my feet, sending Fallon laughing and stumbling a few feet in front of me.

"That's incredible!" Fallon blurted out while the guys and I all shot looks of shock between us. "That show brings some incredible talent, and that means scouts. That's where Regicide Assisted got discovered."

Fallon's face didn't flinch and her smile never faded; her elation and excitement for my band's biggest break was pure and unadulterated. I grabbed her hand, pulling her back toward me. "You're incredible," I whispered.

She wrapped her arms around me and looked back over her shoulder to the guys. "This is going to be your break, guys, I can feel it." Turning back to look at me, she beamed. "I couldn't be happier right now."

"When?" Rodney looked like he was going to puke from the excitement and nerves clashing inside him.

"Three weeks."

Fallon walked over to the couch after grabbing a beer. "Well, boys, I think you better get to playing. We have some work to do."

She giggled and Maverick smiled over to her. "We?"

Fallon nodded. "Yeah, I've been there, done that. Don't you want my professional opinion, for the two cents that it's worth?"

Colt grabbed his guitar, throwing the strap swiftly over his head. "Fuck yeah! Let's do this!"

CHAPTER TWENTY

THE BEGINNING OF AN END

FALLON

The weeks leading up to the Underground Music Fest were crazy and simply amazing. I felt like I had snapped out of my rut and fallen right where I was supposed to be all along. Slowly, everyone except for Dane started calling me Fae. I had decided that I was going to embrace my new life and nickname. I dropped the Dunham and basically was waiting it out for Pearson to take over and make that last piece of my identity puzzle fall into place.

Dane put The Judge in park in front of my apartment building for the last time. "You ready?"

I nodded over at him and we both climbed out of the car. We walked into the office on the second floor of my building and I handed in my keys. The whole process of moving had only taken a few days; since Dane's place was cheaper and closer to work, that's where we decided to call home. And did it ever feel that way.

I was liberated and genuinely happy, but there was still one thing left to do: tell my mom. I had been dragging my feet on even telling her about Dane, let alone that I was about to become his wife, and honestly, I didn't care. She was wrapped up in her life and her marriage and was probably happier without me, or at least not fighting with her husband as much.

As we made our way back into what was now our apartment, I felt like it was time.

"I'm going to call her."

Dane glanced up from the worn out pages of *Loving Mr. Daniels*, which he was reading for the hundredth time. "Want me to go in the other room?"

I shook my head, taking a seat at the dining room table. Nervously, I dialed my mom's cell.

"Hello?" My mom's voice coming from the receiver made goose bumps spread down my arms.

"Hi, Mom. How are you?"

"Fine, sweetheart. It's nice to finally hear from you."

"I know, I'm sorry. I've been really busy with work."

"Tell Payton to cut you some slack from time to time." I could hear my stepfather's voice in the background: "When's dinner?"

"Honey, I need to run. Sam's hungry."

"Mom, wait." It was now or never.

"Yeah?"

"I met someone."

"Oh that's great, sweetie. You'll have to tell me all about him sometime."

"I'm engaged."

A gasp and then silence.

"Mom?"

Sam's voice boomed, "Woman! Get off the damn phone."

"That's wonderful. Have to go. Love you."

Click.

I let my forehead fall onto the cool glass of the table, tears streaming down my face. I felt Dane's hand rest on the back of my head, gently stroking my hair.

"I know the answer, but everything ok?"

I shook my head, more tears falling.

"Come here." Dane pulled me up into his arms, leading me to the couch. We sat, my head on his shoulder, our fingers entangled.

"He's such a bastard."

"What happened?"

"He was just being a prick. He made her get off the phone to cook dinner."

I felt Dane's muscles stiffen at my words. "Should we do something?"

I shook my head. "There's nothing to do. She won't leave him and he doesn't hurt her physically so it's not like I can call the cops."

Dane sighed. "Yeah."

"Listen, if you're not up to it, you—"

I put my finger over his lips; there was no way in hell I was missing his show that night. "I am going and that is final."

My phone buzzed in my pocket with a text.

Starr: Hey bitch, I have a surprise.

Me: What?

Starr: I'm in Chicago.

Me: What the fuck? Where?

Starr: Heading over to the venue with the band our hot roadie is now working for.

Me: What band?

Starr: Don't be mad.

Me: Ok...?

Starr: Lithium. They got added to the lineup for this music fest tonight and I tagged along to hopefully see you.

Me: Kenneth Rhodes is playing tonight at the Underground Music Festival?

Starr: Yeah.

Me: Fuck. So is The Hysterics, Dane's band.

Starr: No fucking way! I'll get to see you!

Me: You can't tell Rhodes about me and Dane or that I'll be there. Promise?

Starr: Yeah, promise. But how are you going to avoid him if you're backstage with The Hysterics?

Me: I'll have to.

Starr: At least I'll get to see you.

Me: Yeah! We're heading that way soon.

Starr: Ok. Love you.

Me: Love you, too.

"Babe? You look like you've seen a ghost."

I looked up at Dane, kissed him on the cheek, and took in a

deep breath. "Starr is in town with Lithium."

"The drug?" Dane smirked, but I shot him a that-is-not-funny look. "Sorry. Your ex's band?"

I nodded.

"And that's a bad thing why? It's not like he knows where you live anymore."

"He's playing the show tonight."

"What?"

I nodded.

"*The* fucking Kenneth Rhodes is going to be playing the same show as my fucking band?" The excitement on Dane's face was understandable but completely infuriating; this was not a good thing. "Why does it matter?"

"Because, I can't see him."

"Then don't see him."

"We'll all be backstage. Someone that knows me might see me."

"So we'll make sure you're discreet. It's going to be fine."

The calmness of Dane's voice was helpful. My heart stopped thumping in my ears and my palms weren't as clammy, but I was still nervous as shit.

"Promise?"

"Babe, I will not let anything happen to you. I can promise you that for sure."

I planted a quick kiss on his plump lips before getting up from the couch. "I love you."

He grabbed my hand, pulling me back down for one more

sweet kiss. "Love you more."

"I'm going to hop in the shower. We need to leave in an hour."

I closed the door to the bathroom behind me, letting the steam fog up the mirror as I searched through the music on my phone to find something that would help me break out of this nervous funk and get back the excitement I needed to help support the guys. I finally stumbled on "Shake It Off" by Taylor Swift and hit play before climbing into the scalding water. I washed and rinsed while bouncing, bobbing, and screaming along to the upbeat tempo of what I decided right then and there needed to be my new theme song.

I toweled off, still humming the catchy beat as Dane peeked his head through the door. "Rocking out in here?"

I nodded, throwing my towel playfully at him as he laughed.

"What?" I questioned.

"You're cute."

I dug through the duffle bag that had most of my clothes in it until I found the perfect shirt to wear. It was a loose-fitting white V-neck with big, bold black letters: I PREFER THE DRUMMER.

After putting on my old style of heavy smoky eye makeup and bright red lipstick, I made sure my curls had enough hairspray in them to last a year. I was ready to go. Dane knocked on the bathroom door, calling in, "Babe, are you ready?"

"Yeah. Coming." I zipped up my tight black leather pants, slipped into my worn out pair of bright red high tops, and made my way into the living room.

Dane slowly walked over to me, a seductive smirk perked up on one side of his mouth. "You look fucking hot." He pulled back my hair to kiss my neck while grabbing my hand. "I guess you don't want to be Fae tonight?"

I kissed his cheek. "I just want to be me. This is me."

"Well then, let's get this show on the road, future wifey."

Flutters.

Weak knees.

I loved the feeling of being completely his. I couldn't wait to be his wife.

"Let's go, babe."

It wasn't until we pulled around the back of the venue into the gated area marked 'restricted' that my nervous jitters started to come back. I tried to take deep, slow breaths while the guys were unloading their equipment backstage, checking all their bags, cases, and boxes to make sure that they hadn't forgotten anything.

I practically jumped out of my skin when I felt someone jump on my back and wrap their arms around my neck "Holy fuck, bitch! I missed you!"

Relief spread through me as Starr's voice registered and I spun around to hug my best friend for the first time in way too long. "It's so good to see you!"

She hadn't changed a bit: short, bright pink hair, purple contacts, eyebrow ring, tight, black corset that made her boobs practically touch her chin. She was a sight for sore eyes, that's for sure. Dane came walking back down the steps to grab the last couple of things from their rent-a-van.

"Babe! Come here!" I called over to him.

"Is that...?" Starr's eyes got wide as Dane wrapped his arm around my shoulders.

"You must be Starr." Dane reached out his hand but Starr threw her arms around his neck and planted a huge, bright pink kiss on his cheek.

I laughed as a confused but amused look danced across Dane's face. "Well," he cleared his throat, "I need to get the last of this stuff."

"Ok, babe. I'll be in soon." Dane nodded and grabbed his stick bag out of the trunk of The Judge.

"Fallon! You didn't tell me how fucking hot he was. He's like walking, talking man candy."

I laughed. "Yeah, I guess he is." I watched as he trotted back up the steps. "So, where is—you know who?"

"Probably off in some bathroom trying to snort as many pills up his nose as he can before he goes on for sound check in fifteen." Starr rolled her eyes as she lit a cigarette. "He's apparently fallen off a damn cliff these last few months."

"That sucks."

"You jumped off a sinking ship, babe. That's for sure."

I nodded. For the first time I didn't feel guilty for leaving my old life. Instead, I felt proud of my decision.

DANE

193

Make sure we have everything, do sound check, find out where the three talent scouts are in the crowd, puke from nerves, see Kenneth Rhodes in the bathroom snorting a years' worth of powder up his nose—check, check, and check.

Finally I was sitting on the counter, sweating bullets in our small dressing room. There were only ten minutes before the first band was supposed to go up. We were fourth in line.

I was tapping my sticks on my knees while Maverick tuned his bass. Fallon was texting someone, presumably Starr.

"Babe, wanna take a walk with me?" Fallon looked up from her phone.

"Yes." Anything to keep my mind a little occupied seemed like an awesome idea.

Hand in hand we made our way down the hall, past musicians, groupies, roadies, and managers. Fallon took me into an empty stairwell and pressed me up against the wall.

"Why are you so nervous?"

"Didn't you hear Colt? There are three scouts here."

She kissed my cheek, whispering in my ear, "And that makes you nervous why?"

I couldn't help but laugh. "Because this is huge for us."

"You're right. But you guys are really talented, don't ever second guess that."

I took in a few deep breaths. "How'd you deal with it?"

"What, nerves?"

I nodded.

"I pretended that the crowd wasn't there. That I was just playing with my friends in my basement."

"That's easier said than done."

She took a step back, pulling my chin down to force eye contact. "You're right. But as long as you're having fun and giving it your all, it's going to be awesome."

I grabbed her shoulders, spun us around and threw her up against the wall. She wrapped her legs around my waist as I crushed our lips together. My hand started riding up her shirt as I kissed down her neck.

Right then we heard stomping behind us and a gruff, slurred voice echoed in the stairwell, "What the fuck is going on here?"

Fallon gasped and pushed away from me, jumping down from my arms. "What the hell are you doing?" she yelled, shifting in front of me.

Kenneth Rhodes was staring at us, his eyes glassed over.

"She asked you a damn question," I barked, about to knock his ass out as I started to lunge out from behind Fallon.

She glanced back at me just fast enough to shake her head and grab my hand, making me wrap her shoulders in my arm as I leaned back against the wall.

"Get the fuck out of here, Kenneth!" she screamed while he stood in the doorway, shaking.

"What the fuck are you doing here with this guy?" His voice was ragged as he steadied himself by leaning against the doorjamb.

"None of your damn business. We're done. Now leave." Fallon's knees and hands were shaking.

"I'm not leaving. How can you fuck some other guy with my baby in you?"

Fallon's entire body tensed. That had been over for what felt like forever, so why was he just bringing it up now? This guy was really fucked out of his skull.

"Kenneth, you have ten seconds to turn around, leave, and never speak to me again or I will kick your teeth in." She seethed.

Kenneth's hands flew into the air. "I am not going anywhere, you fucking bitch! I want to know about the baby!"

Fallon started to explain in a calm deflated voice, "The baby never was. It was a false positive and the only person that knew that I even took a pregnancy test was Starr. So fuck you and leave me alone. I am not having your fucking baby, thank God!"

Without warning, Kenneth lunged at Fallon. I shoved her out of the way, grabbed the collar of his shirt, and started punching him as hard as I could. He stumbled back, blooding pouring from his smiling mouth.

"You're one dead motherfucker." He spit blood onto the floor and then tried to hit me, missing three or four times. I got in a few more clean hits and he was down on the ground.

Fallon got down next to him, smacked his cheeks a few times, and his eyes finally opened. "Kenneth, get the fuck up, you're not that hurt."

In reality, he was pretty banged up. His left eye had a gash over it, one of his teeth had been knocked out, his lip was busted, and both eyes were already showing signs of bruising. Fallon got him to his feet. "We have to get him out of here."

I grabbed his arm, pulling most of his weight onto me, and between the two of us we were able to walk him back to his dressing room.

"Just prop him up here." Fallon started to set him down while he groaned and mumbled in the hallway in front of his dressing room door.

"We can't just leave him here."

He spit blood right onto my shoe. Fallon cocked her head to the side. "His band all knows me. We'll knock and bolt. Someone will help him."

"What if he tells them who did this?"

"He's too fucked up to know what's going on. This isn't the first time something like this has happened to him, trust me."

CHAPTER TWENTY-ONE

MAKE IT OR BREAK IT

FALLON

I slammed the door to The Hysterics' dressing room after Dane and I were safely inside. I was out of breath from sprinting away from Kenneth. We'd left him slumped over, battered and bloody, and I should have felt bad; I didn't. I should have stayed and explained; I couldn't.

Maverick, Colt, and Rodney stared at us while he both heaved, slouched over, hands on our knees.

"What the hell happened to you two?" Maverick handed both of us bottles of water. "We go on in fifteen minutes."

Dane explained what had happened and then looked down at his bloody hands, trying to make a fist with his right. He couldn't.

"Babe? You all right?"

He stared up at me, wide-eyed, shaking his head. "Fuck." He cursed under his breath a few times.

Colt started bouncing around the room. "This is just fucking great. What the hell are we going to do if our drummer can't freaking grip his stick?"

Rodney put his hand on my shoulder. "You have to play the gig."

Dane and I exclaimed in unison, "No!"

My heart was pounding. My mind was racing. My blood was boiling.

I glanced around the room to see the panic in all of the guys' eyes. "You're right. I do."

Dane grabbed my arm with his left hand, "No fucking way. That would out you."

I kissed his cheek. "I can't care about that right now. It's my fault that your hand is broken."

"You didn't make me punch him."

"No, but I'm the reason you were in that stairwell with him. Let me do this."

He pursed his lips and fell onto the couch. "Damn it all to hell. What other choice do we have?"

Maverick sat down next to him. "It's either Fae—ugh, Fallon—plays the show, or we pack up our shit and leave. It is completely up to you. We're in this together, brother."

Rodney and Colt didn't seem too keen on packing up, but they agreed anyway. They really were a family and, for better or worse, they were going to stick by each other.

Someone knocked on the door. "You guys are up in five," a voice called in.

"Let's do this, boys." I grabbed Dane's stick bag and opened

199

the door.

Rodney stopped before exiting the room. "Do I say it's really you?"

"Yes. Why the hell not? They'll figure it out eventually."

"Alright."

One by one they all passed me while I stood frozen in the doorway. Taking a few deep breaths, I followed after them. Dane stopped in front of me and turned around, his face pulled into the saddest frown I had ever seen. "Look, you do not have to do this."

I got up on my tiptoes to kiss him gently. "Yes I do. Everything is going to be fine. I have you and the guys. You are the most important thing in the word to me and I am not going to let your big chance at this band going somewhere fly out the window because of my deadbeat ex."

Dane pulled me into him. "Thank you." He whispered next to my ear, "I love you."

"I love you more."

I got to the side of the stage and everything started to blur together until I was walking up to Dane's set. I had to make a few minor adjustments because of our height differences, and then before I knew it I was sitting on his cushioned stool, gripping a fresh pair of Vic Firth Steve Gadd signature drumsticks. The slick, black wood felt amazing as my entire body shook with adrenaline. Maverick scooted back a little in front on me. "You ready?" he called back.

The crowd was already freaking out and the lights were glaring down on me. I had to be ready so I nodded that I was as Rodney started his introduction. "Ladies, ladies, calm down. We're The Hysterics, and we're here for you. We have a special surprise for you all tonight. Our drummer Dane is out sick and we have a pretty amazing sub for the evening. Please give it up for Fallon Dunbar!"

With that the crowd went ballistic. I half expected to have rotten fruit thrown at my head, but their cheers were pure elation and excitement. We dove right into our set, and just as quickly as it started, Rodney was saying goodnight to the crowd.

We all jogged off the stage and I ran right into Dane's outstretched arms. "You were freaking incredible, babe!" He planted his lips on mine and tears started running down my face.

I was just that freaking happy. A few reporters with press passes tried to get statements from me, but Dane just pushed them away and led me back to our room.

"Fallon! Fallon!"

"Can we get a statement?"

"Why'd you let everyone believe you were dead?"

The band and I got safely into the dressing room and all grabbed waters. I looked down at Dane's hand. "Babe, you need to go to the hospital. I really think that's broken."

His knuckles were bruised, swollen, and bleeding. "Yeah, ok."

Maverick started packing his bass into its case. "Why don't you two get out of here and take care of that? We can handle this stuff."

"You sure?"

Rodney waved us on. "Get out of here, dude! Fallon take care of him, we need that hand to heal up."

I grabbed Dane's good hand and waved goodbye to the guys. "Thanks for trusting me to play for y'all."

Colt laughed. "Thanks for doing it. Fucking Fallon Dunbar just played a gig for us. I still can't believe it."

Dane and I made our way down the back stairs virtually

undetected. As we were walking to The Judge someone shoved me from behind. I spun around to see Starr's pissed off, tear-stained face.

"Dane, please get the car, I need to talk to Starr."

He put light pressure on my shoulder. "Yeah ok."

Starr was seething, shaking as she waited for Dane to walk away.

"How dare you play for them? Fuck you!" Starr was freaking out. I couldn't blame her, but it was all her fault that it happened in the first place.

"You have no right to be mad." I got within an inch of her face.

"Yeah, I sure as heck have *every* goddamn right to be as fucking pissed as I want right now."

"Then explain to me why Kenneth Rhodes tried to attack me and my fiancé because he thought I was pregnant. You're the only one, other than Dane, who knew about that!"

Starr's face went white. "Oh shit."

"Yeah, didn't think that one through, did you?"

She shook her head. "Fallon." She tried to put her hand on my shoulder but I swatted it away.

"Save it. You claim to be my best friend, but you're not. Not anymore."

"Fallon, wait."

I started to walk away from her. Opening the door to The Judge, I turned. "Call me when you grow up." I slammed the door and that was it.

I watched Dane wince as he tried to shift the car.

"Let me drive."

He snorted. "Can you even drive a stick?"

"Yes. Now get the hell out of the driver's seat so I can get you to a doctor."

He reluctantly undid his seatbelt and switched seats with me. I watched Starr stand with her head in her hands as we pulled away from the venue. We turned the corner in silence as my phone lit up with calls and texts from my former bandmates and unknown numbers that I figured were news reporters.

The emergency room trip went by in a whirl of nurses and doctors. Dane had a boxer's fracture. After being scolded for not coming in right away, the doctor immobilized his hand with a splint, gave him some meds for the pain, and we were out the door.

We made our way out of the parking lot and Dane put his hand on my arm while I shifted. "You really are the perfect woman."

I laughed, glancing over at my sappy fiancé. "I love you."

"Love you more."

EPILOGUE

THE INTERVIEW

FALLON

My palms itched as I shuffled around in my seat. There was no turning back; I had to do the interview, but it was the last place on earth I wanted to be.

After the fiasco of the music festival, I knew I was going to have to do a crapload of damage control. I sat fidgeting nervously, hoping that the interview with Colleen Ryder would be enough. Starr and I had barely spoken, it was going to be a while before our relationship got back to normal, but somehow I knew we'd figure it all out. The rest of my former bandmates were understandably pissed, I was getting hate mail from incredibly enraged fans, love notes from sympathetic super fans, and the paparazzi were not leaving me or any member of The Hysterics alone. It had taken just about a month for Dane to convince me that my plan of ordering Chinese takeout and hiding in our apartment for the rest of my life was not a solid one.

The hot lights beamed down on me as the crew finished setting up. The makeup artist placed the last couple of daubs of powder on my face as my interviewer took the chair in front of me.

Colleen Ryder. She was my journalism idol and now she was sitting across from me, notebook in hand, and a sweet, tightlipped smile on her face.

The mics were pinned onto us and she leaned in. "Are you ready?"

I smoothed out my blouse, trying to avoid eye contact. "As ready as I'll ever be."

The cameras started rolling.

Thank goodness this isn't live.

I was sweating. My knee was trying to bounce uncontrollably. My cheeks were hot. My heart was thudding in my ears.

Colleen's strong voice pierced the air, "Good evening, I'm Colleen Ryder and today we have a very special guest with us: Fallon Dunbar, former drummer of Regicide Assisted. Thank you for joining us tonight, Fallon."

"Thank you, Colleen. I wish we were meeting under different circumstances."

The truth was I wished I could go back into hiding and never have to meet Colleen or be in the spotlight at all, but I'd known that possibility had flown out the window right when I'd sat behind that drum set.

"So, Fallon, you pulled the wool over all of our eyes. Why did you assume a new identity and let everyone believe that you had overdosed?"

Straight to the point with this one, no pleasantries or beating

205

around the bush.

"Because I needed to break free from a lifestyle that was killing me."

"Yes, but so many musicians just quit and move on with their lives. Why didn't you think that was a viable option?"

"Do they ever truly live normal lives though? I wanted to be able to walk around without someone trying to take my picture. I wanted to live a normal life."

"I guess none of us can really blame you for that. What made you take the stage that night at the Underground Music Festival?"

"My fiancé Dane, the drummer for The Hysterics, couldn't play, and I didn't want to see all their hard work fly out the window."

"It's rumored that Dane and Kenneth Rhodes got into a fight over you that night. Is that true? Did your fiancé fight your ex because of you that night?"

I took a slow breath in. "Yes, but Rhodes tried to attack me. Dane was just defending me."

"Why would Kenneth Rhodes want to hurt you?"

"Because he was in no shape to even know which way was up. He was clearly not thinking straight that night."

"I see. Well, thankfully he wasn't hurt too badly, just some bruising and a bad cut on his lip. Did you know he was unable to take the stage that night as well?"

I nodded, fighting back tears of frustration. "He wouldn't have been able to sing that night even if he and Dane hadn't fought."

"So, Fallon, let's move on. I hear you're the assistant editor of Raging Underground. How has that been going?"

"It's amazing. The staff is wonderful and I am mostly working from home these days."

"Oh the beauty of technology, right?"

I nodded, smiling shyly. I couldn't tell if she was being nice or condescending.

"I see that beautiful ring on your finger; have you set the date for the wedding?"

Finally, a truly excited smile spread wide on my face. "Actually, we're getting married next week."

"That's soon, isn't it? How exciting."

"The Hysterics start a tour in a few weeks and we wanted to make sure we got married before we leave."

"Well, it has been a pleasure talking with you tonight, Fallon. I am sure everyone will slowly start to come around. Especially with how famous The Hysterics have become these last few weeks."

"It's definitely been an amazing ride. Rough, but amazing."

THE TOUR

DANE

"How're you feeling, baby?"

Fallon shifted in my arms, half-asleep, her sleepy eyes fluttering in the glow from the TV. "Tired," she muttered, nuzzling my neck and kissing me gently before falling back asleep.

I hadn't been sleeping well since our tour started a little over a month back. I felt terrible that Fallon was being dragged along while still having to work remotely for Raging Underground. She was handling it all like a champ, I was just a worrier. The last time she was on tour was her own and she almost didn't live through it. This time was different though; there was so much more to live for.

Channel surfing led me to the Atlanta eleven o'clock news.

"Breaking news!" a young, overly tanned blonde said in her monotone anchor voice. "An Orlando therapist was gunned down in her office this afternoon by one of her patients. Witnesses said they heard a gunshot and then a woman screaming. Candice Davenport was found dead by a patient who had been waiting for her appointment."

The water to the shower turned off and a few minutes later, Rodney came out of the bathroom followed by bellowing steam.

"Hey, Rodney?"

"Yeah, man?" He put on a pair of boxers and crawled into the other queen bed in our room.

"Didn't you date a chick named Candice Davenport?"

He nodded, fluffing his pillows. "Why?"

"She was murdered today by one of her patients. How crazy is that?"

"What? She was planning on going to our show in Tampa in a few weeks. That's insane."

His face showed it all: Rodney wasn't going to talk about it anymore, but it was plain as day. That shit tore him up right on the spot; Rodney was a bleeding heart like that.

"Sorry, man."

He sighed. "I guess that's life. It comes crashing down around you every once in a while."

Fallon rolled back over into me and grabbed my hand. "Feel." She pressed my hand onto her belly. "Leilani is restless tonight."

I stared down at the most beautiful woman in the world as I felt our baby kick inside her. It was so true: life did have a way of crashing down around you, but that isn't always a bad thing.

I kissed the top of Fallon's head. "I love you," I whispered, pulling her closer to me.

She kissed my cheek. "Love you more."

the end.

BONUS:

A DELETED SCENE

FALLON

"Fallon?"

I rolled over to see Dane sitting up, gripping my open journal. "What's that?" I muttered, trying to play dumb. Why? I had no idea.

Pulling up the sheet to cover my bare chest, my eyes darted from his to the leather bound pages that bore my soul.

He swallowed hard. "It was open on the floor. I'm sorry but I read the page it was open to. You're an amazing writer."

I took the book from his hands, running my fingers over the pressed paisley pattern. "I used to write all the lyrics for the band. It's part of the reason they broke up; the words ran dry."

"What the fuck do you mean you're done?" Starr barked at me while she paced in my parents' kitchen.

I could barely even sit up straight I was so weak from my weekend of puking and withdrawals. "I mean, this is my one chance to get clean, but to do that I have to be done with the band, Starr. I'm sorry."

Letting my head fall to the table, I stared up at my raging best friend while tears started to pour from her honey eyes. "I just don't get it. Go to rehab, sure. That makes sense. But don't give up on everything we've worked so fucking hard for. How much more selfish can you be?"

"It is selfish, but it's do this and save my life, or let the underground swallow me whole and risk not making it out alive next time. I should be fucking dead, is that what you want?"

"You might as well be dead, you fucking bitch! I wish you were!"

"Fallon?" Dane's voice broke into my flashback. "You ok?"

I shook my head rapidly and opened my journal to a page I knew Dane hadn't read, the last words I had scribbled before my writer's block hit a few days before. "Can I read you something?"

He nodded and I cleared my throat while my eyes scanned the page, swallowing the nagging nerves that were starting to thump in my chest. Eventually I read, with a shaking voice and an exposed heart.

Let the world know you're a spark

A catalyst in one hand and detonation the other

Bring them together and you can light up this place

Let yourself go and you could destroy this space

Be the change your makeup has run for

Be the one thing that hasn't been done before

Walk in the shoes you've been destined to fill

Don't let this just rest on others' will

There is an explosion bottled up inside

Let the fuse sizzle and just enjoy the ride

I paused and waited, taking deep breaths, hoping that Dane would speak soon.

"I have to say that's not something that I was expecting." He pulled the book from my hand, pressing his lips softly to mine.

"Why?" I pushed away from him and leaned against my padded gray headboard.

"It's not as dark as I thought it would be. It's so..." While he paused to find the words, my heart pounded. I had never worried that someone would dislike my writing; usually my mentality was to just say 'fuck it' and not even care if someone thought it was pitiful dribble.

"It's ok, you can say it sucked." I nudged his shoulder and he grabbed my arm, pulling me to him. His bare muscles flexed under my weight as he shifted me on top of him.

"Don't put words in my mouth. I was trying to find a better word for hopeful. The writing screams hope. It's brilliant."

SNEAK PEEK:

STUPID HEARTS

AN EROTIC NOVELLA
KRISTEN HOPE MAZZOLA

CHAPTER 1.

Well, crap.

Got home from a long ass shoot in Virginia Beach at the ass crack of dawn after a terrible flight full of turbulence and a screaming baby. Made sure Dozer was all settled in, filled up his food and water bowls, fluffed his oversized bed in the living room, and made sure that he was happily gnawing on a gigantic rawhide. Finally took a deep breath as I slipped off my favorite dark brown and black ostrich boots.

I slunk into my closet-sized bathroom. It looked like Pepto-Bismol had puked all over the damn thing. From the tiles to the bathtub and even the toilet, it was saturated in the awful pink color. The pipes complained loudly until steaming hot water bellowed from the faucet.

I stripped off my typical black loose fitting V-neck and skintight black skinny jeans then stood staring at my tired eyes in the mirror. The curls had fallen out of my hair a while ago and the makeup I'd applied at four in the morning was smudged and faded. I looked like a freaking train wreck standing like a Looney Tunes character in my underwear. I peeled off my black lace bra and matching thong and sank into a much needed scalding hot bath to relax.

After toweling off, throwing my long dark brown locks into a messy dripping bun, and slipping into my pajamas at eleven o'clock in the morning, the only thing left to do was unpack my carryon bag.

By far my least favorite part of the whole traveling for work thing was living out of a suitcase. Oh, and the never ending laundry once I finally got home.

It was a typical Monday morning for me until I started to go through the zipped pocket of my suitcase where I normally stowed all of my intimates, including my pink bullet vibrator. What the hell did I find?

Nothing.

All of my favorite thongs were gone. All of my beautiful lace bras that matched those thongs were gone. Devastation set in fast when I realized my favorite vibrator, the one that had been on the road with me for the past three years, was gone.

Well crap!

After three hours of no luck complaining about the travesty of my stolen intimates to anyone that picked up the phone, I slumped onto the couch to stew in a pissed off channel surfing escapade to mourn the loss of my battery powered o-maker.

My phone buzzed on the light wood coffee table, next to where my bare feet were resting—an unknown eight-hundred number.

I answered, "This is Jolene."

An automated voice came on the line. "Hello. It has come to our attention that you were dissatisfied with our customer service regarding luggage handling. Please hold for a customer service operator."

Fester. Fester. Fester. At that point my blood was boiling and I was ready to bite the head off of this customer service operator.

"Hello. This is Maureen. It appears that you placed a complaint call earlier today. Please confirm your name for me?"

"Jolene Abbott."

"Thank you, Ms. Abbott. How are you doing today?"

She seemed so sweet. Her vanilla coated voice cooed into the phone, but I didn't give a rat's ass. I seethed, "You want to know how the hell I am doing? I get home from my business trip to find that some pervert that works for y'all in baggage handling gets off on stealing women's intimates. Now I am left with none of my nice underwear or my favorite vibrator! Yes, I did just say vibrator! And y'all won't do a damn thing because there isn't a record of anyone searching my bag. Of course the perv didn't leave a damn record of his sick little game and of course y'all won't help me. So I'm sorry, Maureen. I know you're just doing your job, but I am freaking pissed and y'all either need to reimburse me for the personal property that was stolen from me or just leave me the heck alone."

There was a brief pause.

Maybe I was too harsh?

Finally her sweet voice, which was a little softer now, came back on the line. "I'm very sorry to hear that ma'am. I can transfer you to my supervisor. He might be able to help you."

"Fuck this." Click.

I threw on a Lynyrd Skynyrd shirt and a pair of faded gray skinny jeans, slid my socked feet back into my boots, and applied a light layer of eyeliner and mascara to avoid looking completely dead.

Tossing my phone into my purse, I gave Dozer a few kisses on his egg shaped head. "Be back in a bit, bud." His whip-like tail thumped against the plush bed as I walked to the door. Right as I pulled my bag's strap over my shoulder and opened the front door, he closed his eyes.

Typical. I shrugged and started to make my way down the ten flights of stairs.

Time to go shopping.

A successful Victoria's Secret trip was not all that I had planned for this shopping excursion. I hailed a cab, hopped in, and without giving it a second thought, I instructed the cabby to take me to "Seventh Avenue South and Charles Street, please."

"Alright." He grinned at me through the rearview mirror, eying my pink striped bag, showing off his lack of teeth along with the ones he did have left, which were stained piss-yellow and looked to be hanging on by a thread.

Gross.

I slid out of the cab at the end of the block and made my way to The Pleasure Chest. The faded red brick exterior and the light gray awning did not do the sexual wonderland justice.

A bell chimed overhead as I was greeted by a rather large

middle-aged woman. She was covered in tattoos and leaning on the front counter, looking bored out of her skull.

"How can I help please you today?"

The greeting made me giggle. "I have come because of a travesty."

She gasped and came around the counter to help comfort me in my devastated state. "What happened?" She softly put her pudgy hand onto my shoulder.

"My Iconic Bullet was stolen!"

The woman gasped again, louder this time, and threw her hand to her chest. "Well let's find you a new pocket-sized boyfriend."

I grinned and followed her to the back wall, past the sexy role-playing costumes, anal plugs, and strap-ons.

"Now, you might like something like this?" She held up a white ball that looked like it was wearing a weird pink crown.

Nope!

"That is interesting," I faked, not wanting to hurt her feelings. "What's it called?"

"This one is the Vibratex Girls Princessa. My husband loves to roll it around on my clit while I'm climaxing."

Way too much information.

I grabbed a LoveLife Discover from the wall and read its specs: *Discover the pleasure of this versatile mini vibe! Made of silicone and USB rechargeable, this sweet little vibrator has seven delicious settings and is perfect for travel or for a not-so-quiet night in.*

Pink. Simple. My kind of thing.

"I think this is the one."

She nodded and within a few minutes I was curbside, trying

to hail another taxi to take me home. A cab finally pulled up and right as I was going for the handle, another hand got there first.

"Excuse me, this is my cab," I barked, turning to the owner of the rude hand.

I was greeted by stunning ice blue eyes, a strong, stubble-covered jawline, and a huge toothy grin.

"Sorry." His voice was deep and velvety, matching his five thousand dollar suit well. He started to back away from the cab and I panicked. I needed to see more of those eyes so I blurted out, "We could share? I'm heading to the Upper East Side."

He nodded. "So am I."

We hopped in and I gave the directions to my overly expensive apartment at fifth and seventy-sixth, where my one room studio overlooked Central Park.

My cab-mate chuckled.

"Was something I said funny to you, sir?" I drawled at him in the most southern bell voice I could muster.

"It's not every day that a bohemian looking southerner lives in an area of town like that."

"Excuse me?"

"Forgive me, but you don't look like you'd live there."

The cab stopped in front of my building and I got out, slamming the door shut without so much as a backwards glance at the asshat that I'd had the misfortune of sharing a cab with. Beautiful or not, an asshat is an asshat, and I was not going to take shit from someone like that.

"Miss?"

I heard his husky voice call from the parked cab and the door shut behind him.

"What?" An exasperated tone escaped me as I turned to meet his stunning eyes and a cruel smile raking across his lips.

"You left this in the cab."

To my horror, he was holding my new toy in his hand.

All kinds of red danced across my face as I took my vibrator from him. "Thanks," I choked, gulping the last bit of saliva out of my drying mouth.

"Want to have drinks later?"

I was rather taken aback by his question. "What?"

"I'm only in town a few nights a month and I leave in the morning. I'm free after my next meeting and would love to have some company at the hotel lounge instead of drinking by myself."

He handed me a business card with an address scribbled on the back. "That's where I am staying. I'll be in the lobby around eight. See you there if you'd like."

He got back in the cab while I stood like an idiot, grasping his card in one hand, my vibrator and lingerie bag in the other.

What a freaking weird day!

STUPID HEARTS

AN EROTIC NOVELLA

BY KRISTEN HOPE MAZZOLA

AVAILABLE NOW TO ORDER!

DID YOU ENJOY WHAT YOU JUST READ?

RATE IT: If the answer is yes, you did enjoy Falling Back Together, please consider putting up a review on **Amazon**, **Goodreads**, or **Barnes and Noble**.

SHARE IT: Please help spread the word about The Hysterics. Tell your friends and family about it or share it with them. Sharing is caring, after all.

STAY CONNECTED: Follow Kristen Hope Mazzola on **facebook.com/authorkristenhope** or **twitter.com/khmazz** to stay up to date about new releases, giveaways, and so much more!

All books by
Kristen Hope Mazzola

The Crashing Series:

Crashing: The Wedding: Cali's Story

(Crashing #0.5) (a standalone prequel to the Crashing Series)

Crashing Back Down (Crashing #1)

Falling Back Together (Crashing #2)

Standalones:

The Hysterics

Stupid Hearts

Unacceptable: A Stepbrother Romance

Rough & Tumble

SPECIAL THANKS

TO MICHAEL: I know that I've said it a thousand times, but thank you for showing me that soulmates do exist, that they aren't mythical creatures and thank you for being mine. I love you.

TO DAYNA: Holy crap! This has been one hell of a wild ride. Thanks for not giving up on these characters and me! Without your support, unwavering friendship, and your honesty, even if it was brutal at times, this book would never have been finished. I really could not have written this, or any book, without you by my side!

TO BRITTAINY C. CHERRY, AUTHOR OF *LOVING MR. DANIELS*: You are the best book bestie a girl could ever have! I cannot count how many times you have talked to me off the ledge. Thank you for not letting me give up! I really owe you for that!

TO BRITTANY JO JAMES, AUTHOR OF *THE REBELS*: You are complete and total sunshine – that is really the only way I can describe how beautiful and sweet you are! I love our chats and how positive you always are. Never stop believing in your abilities, and please never let me stop believing in mine.

TO MY DAD: Thanks for being the first rock star I ever loved and for teaching me to always follow my dreams, no matter how big or small they are. You will always be my number one fan and I will always be yours. By the way, you're the most talented drummer I have ever seen, so thanks for helping spark the inspiration for this book, The Hysterics would have never been written if it wasn't for you.

TO DIESEL: (Yes, I have my dog in here) Thanks for grunting, barking, growling, shoving, and stressing me out from under my desk. I really needed those breaks from time to time. For anyone that has, had or knows a bull terrier, I'm sure you understand this one.

TO MY AMAZING EDITOR, C MARIE: Girl, you freaking rock and I am so thankful to work with someone as talented and good-hearted as you are. You are so positive and respectful, and I really value you as my colleague and thank you for helping my writing skills improve.

TO CHRISTINE AND LEA FROM *THE HYPE PR*: Holy hell, I do not know what I would do without either of you! Thank you for having my back and believing in me!

TO EVERY MEMBER ON MY STREET TEAM: You all are freaking amazing and I don't know what I would do without your support! Thank you for believing in me!

Lastly, thank you from the bottom of my heart to the entire book world. To every member from authors, bloggers, readers, editors, cover models and designers and everyone else in between, we have built up an amazing community of support and passion for the written world, one that I am so honored to be a part of.

NOTE FROM THE AUTHOR

Thank you for buying my novel. In doing so, you have helped fulfill a very important goal of mine. From every purchase of any of my books, I donate to the Marcie Mazzola Foundation. The mission of the foundation is to "help better the lives of abused and at-risk children; and to build community awareness regarding the needs of children."

The Marcie Mazzola Foundation was established in 2003 by my family. On July 6, 2002, Marcie died tragically in an automobile accident. Although she was only 21 at the time of her death, Marcie had experienced many things and touched many lives. She was a beautiful young woman whose inner beauty surpassed even her physical beauty because of her compassionate nature and treatment of others.

At the time of her death, Marcie was involved in a civil lawsuit against a school bus driver who had sexually abused her when she was 11 years old. Prior to her death, it had been expected that the case would be won, but since Marcie could no longer testify, it was going to be next to impossible to win. Marcie's attorney met with her family to determine if the suit should be continued. He advised the family that Marcie had confided in him her intention to donate her entire award to help sexually and physically abused children if she won the case. Once this was known, the family had no doubt that the suit had to continue.

The attorney's strong commitment to Marcie prompted him to proceed with the case, and against all odds, it was won. Marcie's estate was awarded a monetary settlement. With her attorney's guidance and continued support, the family established a foundation as a tribute to Marcie's life, which would continue her legacy to help children.

To learn more about The Marcie Mazzola Foundation, please visit: http://www.marciemazzolafoundation.org

Marcie Mazzola Foundation
158 Burr Road, Commack, NY 11725
phone: 631-858-1855 • fax: 631-462-8544
email: info@marciemazzolafoundation.org

THE AUTHOR

Hi! I am just an average twenty-something following my dreams. I have a full time "day job" and by night I am an author. I guess you could say that writing is like my super power (I always wanted one of those). I am a lover of wine, sushi, football and the ocean; that is when I am not wrapped up in the literary world.

Please feel free to contact me to chat about my writing, books you think I'd like or just to shoot the, well you know.

Stay Connected:

KristenHopeMazzola.com

https://www.facebook.com/AuthorKristenHope

https://goodreads.com/author/show/7179522.Kristen_Hope_Mazzola

https://twitter.com/khmazz

Email: authorkristenmazzola@gmail.com